Readers love the Thornwood
series by CAITLIN RICCI

One More Time

"I had a blast with this story… It caught my attention from the
moment I started reading and kept it all the way to the end."
—MM Good Book Reviews

"It was excellently written, and Caitlin makes sure not to
rush…"
—Just Love: Romance Novel Reviews

About Last Night

"Once I started this little gem, I couldn't stop until I finished."
—Inked Rainbow Reads

"I am in awe of this book, the character development is
beautiful."
—Two Chicks Obsessed

By CAITLIN RICCI

Blood Slave
Country Strong
For the Asking
His Lion Tamer
Marked by Grief
One Pulse (Dreamspinner Anthology)
Reckless
With Cari Z: Worth the Wait

A FOREVER HOME
Rescuing Jack
Of Monsters and Men

A PLANET CALLED WISH
To the Highest Bidder
Fantasy for a Gentleman
Falling Into the Black

THORNWOOD
One More Time
About Last Night
Somewhere to Belong

With Kara Nash
DARE
Dare to Risk
Dare to Hope

Published by DREAMSPINNER PRESS
www.dreamspinnerpress.com

By CAITLIN RICCI (CONT.)

Published by Harmony Ink Press
Crush
First Time for Everything (Harmony Ink Anthology)
With A.M. Burns: Running with the Pack

ROBBIE & SAM
Weathering the Storm
Head Above Water
Battle Born

Published by DREAMSPINNER PRESS
www.dreamspinnerpress.com

Somewhere *to* Belong

Caitlin Ricci

Published by
DREAMSPINNER PRESS

5032 Capital Circle SW, Suite 2, PMB# 279, Tallahassee, FL 32305-7886 USA
www.dreamspinnerpress.com

Somewhere to Belong
© 2017 Caitlin Ricci.

Cover Art
© 2017 Caitlin Ricci.
Cover Design
© 2017 Paul Richmond.
http://www.paulrichmondstudio.com
Cover content is for illustrative purposes only and any person depicted on the cover is a model.

ISBN: 978-1-63533-588-0
Digital ISBN: 978-1-63533-589-7
Library of Congress Control Number: 2017904539
Published August 2017
v. 1.0

Printed in the United States of America
∞
This paper meets the requirements of
ANSI/NISO Z39.48-1992 (Permanence of Paper).

CHAPTER ONE

Eli

A ROCK held the door slightly open to hotel room 221, just as PendletonGray had promised it would be. The lights were on, and I smiled at him as I leaned against the door to close it behind me. The lock clicked on its own, and I quickly began stripping off my T-shirt and tossing it onto a nearby chair. PG, as I'd taken to thinking of him over the past two months since we'd first started hooking up, lay stretched out on the bed with a sheet over his lap. It was bunched up to expose as much of his dark skin as he possibly could while still being at least a little modest, which wasn't needed around me since I'd seen him naked about a half-dozen times now, but maybe he'd done it just in case one of the cleaning crew had come by and peeked into the open room.

"Hey," I said as I kicked off my sneakers and then pulled down my tight jeans. They were special jeans meant to ride in, but he didn't know that I rode horses. He didn't know anything about me, actually. I was naked under them, and I pulled a condom out of the back pocket of my jeans before joining him on the bed.

"Did you have any trouble finding the hotel?"

PG liked to change the location of our hookups each time, but they were always in a hotel, and always a really nice one too. We could have just gotten together at any cheap motel, or in the back of my car like the other guys I screwed from the app we both used. But he was classier than that.

I shook my head. "Golden isn't that far from me, so it was easy." He didn't know where I lived. I could have been lying, and I kind of was, depending on his definition of close. I'd driven over an hour from Castle Rock to get to him today, but I knew he was always worth it, so I didn't even think twice about agreeing to be with him when his request had come in.

He moved the sheet aside, exposing his thick cock and the soft patch of dark hair at its base. I was pretty free from hair, without even trying, but I was also twenty-five. If I had to guess, PG was somewhere in his late forties or early fifties, judging by the trace bits of gray in his short black curls. I slid over his lap, and he settled his hands loosely on my hips. While I smiled at him, I let his tip kiss my entrance before I moved my hand there and removed my plug. I tossed it off the bed to be retrieved later.

He didn't look surprised by me having one in. He shouldn't have been either after knowing me in this capacity for so many months. "How long were you wearing it this time?"

"Three days." PG didn't ask me if that had been three days straight minus bathroom breaks, probably because he knew me better than that. I generally didn't go more than a day without meeting someone from the app, and since my profile was public, anyone who was curious enough would have been able to see my activity.

He tightened his fingers on my bony hips, and I felt the eagerness coursing through him. I had been looking at his profile too, and I knew he'd been busy, just as I had been, so it was nice to know that I was still wanted. I made quick work of spreading the lubricated condom over his cock. Sliding onto him was easy since I'd been stretched already. That was one way I controlled these hookups. Since I was always ready, there was no way anyone could go too fast with me.

I ground into him, moving my hips until I found the right angle and pace that worked for me. After months of seeing him, I knew this was how we did things. When he was on the bed, I rode him, and I got to find my climax all on my own. Sometimes it felt like I was using him as I slapped our bodies together and knew I wasn't giving him what he wanted. But it never took long for me to come, as I rested one hand on his chest and wrapped the other around my cock, which had been painfully hard while I'd thought about him on the highway up there.

I whimpered as I fought back my orgasm and tried to hang on just a little while longer. I should have jacked off before getting in my car. Then maybe I would have lasted more than a few minutes with his cock rubbing perfectly against my prostate in the most delicious way possible. But PG sent me over the edge as he moved his hands from my hips and reached up to tug on my nipples. A bit of pain was my thing. Not anything hardcore, but just enough to send that zap of energy coursing through me. It was a bit of a shock, since I was never sure how he was going to give me that extra bit of a boost, but he usually did.

PG grabbed my ass and turned me over while I was still coming down from my climax, which had ended up all over his chest and stomach. He pressed my knees back against my chest with his shoulders and slammed into me while I was still limp under him. Unlike a lot of guys, he didn't say someone else's name while he was fucking me. He generally didn't say anything at all. Just a bunch of grunts and groans to let me know he was enjoying me as much as I loved having him.

He kissed me as I lay under him. It was the only time we ever kissed. He was needy and rough, biting my lips with his teeth as he panted into the kisses. Once I had control of my hands again, I brought my fingers up and ran them through his hair. His tight curls were coarse but also soft at the ends. Like he used some expensive conditioner but it had become less effective this late in the evening. It was nearly eight o'clock.

He met my gaze a second before he came with a loud groan, and though I would never tell him, I liked seeing the vulnerability in his dark brown eyes as he climaxed. He'd come, so he stopped kissing me. He pulled out, tossed the condom aside, and rolled away from me all within a few seconds.

We lay there together for a while, just panting and trying to catch our breaths. I was the first to get up. I went to my plug, washed it off, and put it back in with the help of some lube I kept on me at all times, then pulled on my jeans. They were harder to get on than they had been to take off because I was so sweaty, but I managed them anyway. When I put my feet in my sneakers, I found PG watching me with a smile on his face. He'd moved the pillows behind his head, propping himself up a little.

"You know you can stay and shower here, right?" he asked me.

I shrugged before I pulled on my shirt. "Yeah. I know. You've told me that before. But I'm good. Not staying around isn't just a thing I do with you." I'd learned better than to be clingy in the few years since I'd started using the app to get my needs taken care of. I just wanted to go.

PG chuckled and sat up in bed. He really did look good naked. He'd taken care of himself well, and as he stood up and headed toward the bathroom, he walked with grace and none of the clumsiness I was used to seeing from guys my age.

"Are we to the first name stage yet? It's been months since we've been getting together after all."

I wasn't sure. Maybe we were. I figured there was no harm in him knowing just that much about me. "Eli."

"Grayson."

Which meant that his full name might have been Grayson Pendleton, judging by his screenname on Hot Guy Hook Ups.

Not that I cared. His name made him sound rich and powerful. Maybe he was some kind of secret billionaire who liked doing the hookup thing on the side. What he did or didn't do really didn't matter to me. He was sexy, and I liked coming with him. That was it.

"See you," I said. I waved to him as I backed away toward the door. This part was always a bit awkward for me. Come in, get naked, have sex. Those were the parts I could handle. This afterward part where he told me I could shower and now we knew each other's names? That was weird. I liked my sex somewhere between strangers and glory holes. I hoped Grayson wasn't going to start wanting to get to know me or anything like that. I didn't do that anymore. My lines were definitely drawn far before we would ever get to be anything close to friends.

He smiled at me again. "Take care. I'll message you the next time I'm in town."

"Sounds like a plan." I ducked out of the hotel room as I heard him turning on the shower.

Sex generally made me feel better, looser, and far more energized. If it wasn't a Wednesday night, and if I didn't have a home evaluation for the horse rescue I worked for in the morning, I would have probably gone to a club. As it was, I headed back to my apartment, which was stupid expensive, and now that my year lease was up in two weeks, I was sure that the owner was going to be increasing the rent once I went month-to-month.

It wasn't a prospect I was looking forward to since I could barely afford to live there as it was. But rent was skyrocketing all over the Denver Metro Area, and even though I'd looked for a cheaper place, they didn't exist unless I wanted a roommate. Which I definitely didn't. They came with complications. I'd fallen hard for every guy I'd ever tried to share a place with, and that just couldn't be me anymore.

I lived on the ground-level apartment, and I lived alone, unless the pictures of horses counted. Then I had fifty-two friends, all horses that I'd either helped rescue from bad situations or placed into good homes. I had a few human friends too, but not ones who generally came to my apartment. We hit the gay clubs in downtown Denver together or hung out at the barn after work. But we didn't really all get together at my place and drink beers and watch a football game or anything like that.

I stripped off my shirt and tossed it into my overflowing laundry basket in the hall between my bedroom and the bathroom, where my washer and dryer were, before plopping down on my thrift store sofa. It was cheap, but it was comfortable. My water bottle from the night before was still on the floor, next to the sofa, and I sipped it as I thought about Grayson. I was already getting hard again, and I groaned as I rolled over onto my stomach and tried to ignore my body's reaction to one of the hottest men I'd ever had sex with.

I had to get up early in the morning and do a home evaluation in Kiowa. I had to be there by eight, then was scheduled to be at the rescue for four hours after that since I had paperwork and monthly checks to do. I didn't have any more time to spend thinking about Grayson that night. Only my brain didn't seem to want to accept that.

It sucked that I didn't have more control of my body than this, but I was already practically humping the couch while thinking about having him in me again. Unlike most guys, he'd never disappointed me when we were together. Some guys were good, but then they had an off night, and I still gave them another chance. Two bad times in a row meant I didn't see them again. Which was probably why most of the guys I was with didn't get to repeat their times with me.

But Grayson was different. I rolled back over and undid my jeans so that I could put my fist around my cock. I arched into my hand and groaned as I thought about how rough he liked to be with me when he pinned me down to a bed or pushed me up against a wall. I wanted him to fuck me as hard as he could, and he never shied away from that. We were sweaty and loud, and we'd broken more than one hotel headboard. My best times were with him for sure.

I thought about his fingers on my hips, then when he pinched my nipples. Or the times when he'd dug his nails into the outside of my thighs as I'd ridden him. He was good about always letting me come first. And when I was done was when he really got started. While I lay there loose and relaxed, he took me, and I loved it all.

I jerked my hand over my cock and shot over my stomach while I imagined him on top of me, kissing me as if he needed me, like he always did right before he came. When I was done, and filthy again, I was finally able to get some sleep.

CHAPTER TWO

Grayson

I FLIPPED through my phone while waiting for my plane to arrive. Just three days in Colorado and I was already scheduled to leave again. As depressing as that sometimes was, I was used to it by now. I opened the app and scrolled through my messages. Guys wanting to see me again, guys wanting to get a chance with me for the first time. Members could rate each other, and my rating was pretty high, which was flattering, but made a lot of guys I'd never even considered bringing into my bed suddenly want me in the most desperate ways possible.

The one person I didn't have a message from was Eli. That wasn't surprising, since he never sent me a message to begin with, but it still unnerved me somewhat. I was used to keeping in contact with the guys I saw regularly, and some of them had even become sort of friends. Not the kind I would go out with in public or want to see in a nonsexual situation, but they were men that I could have a conversation with after we were done screwing each other. I had thought Eli and I would be at that point somewhere over the past few months, but he seemed determined to keep me at arm's length. I couldn't believe it had taken so long for me to even get his name. I'd been asking him for that information since the first time we'd been together.

Normally I only messaged him when I wanted to see him, but since we knew each other's names now, I thought perhaps saying hi would be appropriate. I sent off the message and kept scrolling through my notices. I was headed to Cleveland, to help a bank CEO restructure his toptier employees. I was scheduled to be gone for a week, but I intended for the job to last only a few days. I'd go through the employee files on the first day, conduct interviews with those employees I thought could be cut on the second, and give my final results to the CEO on the third day. With that in mind, I started looking through my regular contacts to see if anyone might be available during that time for a quick hookup. If not I could search by city and find someone, but when I was doing a job, I preferred to have the guys I was comfortable with around me. One of my biggest fears was hooking up with someone and then running into them the next day while I was doing my job, so I always tried to schedule something on the last night that I would be in town. It also worked because I would never have time to do a second date right away with them like some guys thought I should.

Eli messaged me back while I was deciding between two guys I'd been with the year before. They were both in their thirties, well educated, and great in bed—my type to a tee. Out of everyone I was with regularly, Eli was the one who didn't fit into that mold. He was in his twenties and listed no educational history in his profile. Maybe that was to keep some part of his life private, which I guessed, but most guys boasted about whatever Ivy League college they'd attended. Eli wasn't like that at all.

Hey his message simply said. Still, it made me smile.

What are you doing right now? I sent back to him.

Within seconds I received another message from him, this time with a picture attached to it. In it I saw him with someone's cock shoved deep into his mouth, and there was already come on his cheek and around his lips as if he was cleaning the guy off instead of just getting down to it. I was instantly hard, and I needed to go adjust myself. How one picture of Eli, especially of him being with someone else, could make me that needy so quickly was beyond me. Maybe it was because I knew how good he was with his mouth and all the little sounds he made when he was on his knees in front of someone that did it for me.

I thought he would expect me to say something, but I wasn't sure what to say to a picture like that. He'd never shared something like that with me. I'd known he was with other people. We weren't exclusive or dating in any sense of the word, but I'd never seen him with anyone before, and the image in my mind that I now couldn't shake was of him going down on someone and me getting to watch him do it. I didn't have time to find a bathroom and take care of my needs, and part of me wanted to be angry at him for putting me in the position where I'd be hard for a flight from Denver to Cleveland all because of him, but I couldn't make myself blame him for sharing the picture with me at all. *It looks like you're having fun*, I started off my message to him. *I'm on my way to Cleveland*. I didn't bother wondering why there was a sudden change in him, from finally telling me his name to sending me a sexy pic of himself with someone else. I accepted these things, like I accepted everything else about Eli. He was a mystery, and one I wanted to know more about, but I was in no desperate rush to invade his personal life with my curiosity.

The next message he sent me included another selfie, but this time just of his face and totally cleaned up. He was blowing me a kiss, something he hadn't done since our first time together and he'd said goodbye to me at the hotel door. *See you when you get back.*

I smiled and sent him another message. It would be the last one for the day, since they'd started boarding and I was about to get on the plane. *Of course. Take care.*

I turned my phone off and put it back in my briefcase before heading onto the airplane.

THREE DAYS in Cleveland had me ready to come home. I was thanked for my work, the CEO shook my hand, and I was back on a plane to return home to Colorado the next day. I'd met up with two guys in my three days in Cleveland, both of them perfectly fine in their own ways, but I was hardly enthusiastic about either of them.

Getting back to Colorado, where I'd been born and raised, was always pleasant, but returning to my recently inherited house in the Rocky Mountains was not. I hadn't been close to my father and hadn't spoken to him in at least ten years. I hadn't even known that he was sick before he died. But he'd left me a three-bedroom house in Thornwood, and out of the blue, I found myself with a property I'd never been to in a town I'd never heard of.

It wasn't a bad place to call home, if I ever got around to that point with the house. As it stood now, I was indifferent to it. Having a house that was paid off was nicer than having to pay rent, but the house felt sterile whenever I walked through the front door. It was cold and often covered in dust. I'd unpacked my boxes, what few I had since I was never in one place long enough to really accumulate much. I didn't have anything in my kitchen since I hated to cook for just myself. But this wasn't Denver with its many restaurants and bars. There was only one restaurant in Thornwood, which was a diner, and I greatly disliked greasy diner food.

With a sigh I settled into my favorite chair, the only piece of furniture I'd brought over from my place in Denver, and contemplated the Italian takeout I'd purchased on the way from Denver International Airport to Thornwood. It had been over an hour's drive, and though the restaurant I'd stopped at was one of my regular favorites, the idea of heating up my pasta primavera in the old microwave was not at all tempting. Instead I turned to my phone and began browsing through the app. I didn't exactly want someone right then. But talking to someone might have been nice. Eli had been active within the past forty-five minutes according to the app. Maybe I could interest him in going out to dinner with me. *I'm back in town. Can I take you to dinner?* I messaged him.

Can't. Sorry.

I frowned down at his nearly instantaneous message. *Are you busy? I could wait.* For most guys I wouldn't have bothered, but Eli's refusal to let me get emotionally close to him had intrigued me from the beginning. A few hours with him when we weren't having sex right away might have been just the treat I needed to break me out of the work-travel funk I'd slipped into since coming home.

I don't go out with the people I screw. Sorry.

Well, that was incredibly blunt, especially for him, since he rarely said anything to me. *I see.* I was just a hookup to him. Which made sense. But in a way it also shed a different sort of light on any potential friendship I might have been able to find with him. I wondered what about me he found objectionable beyond someone to spend an hour or so with. Perhaps it was my age. I was a few decades older than him after all. Or maybe it was that I was black and he was very Midwest farm boy.

I'll be free in a few days. I hadn't expected another message so soon from him, and especially not one where he initiated us getting together. That was never our way. I messaged him for a meeting. He was never the one to reach out to me. Until now. It was strange, and I wanted to know why he was changing that part of our dynamic as well.

But did I want to see him anymore, given that I knew he had no interest in seeing me with my clothes on? The answer was a resounding yes. Whatever his reasons for not wanting to be anything more than sexual partners was, that didn't diminish the times we spent together. *I will contact you then. Good night.*

His answer came a few seconds later. *Night.*

CHAPTER THREE

Eli

I HAD the day off, so I'd been lounging in a pair of track pants all day while binge-watching Netflix and eating popcorn for all of my meals. It had been a great day, until the son of my apartment manager came knocking on my door.

"Hey," he said once I'd opened it.

"Can I help you?" His name was Billy, or Bobby, maybe Brent. Something with a *B*. I hadn't really paid attention much. He did landscaping around the apartment complex, and once in a while, he was the maintenance man if his dad couldn't make a call or was busy or something.

He smiled at me and leaned against the doorframe, halfway putting himself in my apartment. "I wanted to let you know that your rent will be increasing by three hundred a month starting on the first. You'll get a notice in the mail telling you that too."

I'd been afraid of that. "Well, that sucks. Thanks for the heads-up and all, but really, it sucks ass."

His smile turned sharper then, becoming far more predatory and dangerous. I held my ground and didn't back away, but I knew from years spent in the club when I was being sized up and when someone was interested in me.

"Don't I know you from the app?"

He probably did. Most of the gay guys that I knew had used it at least once. More often than not, though, they were weekly users. I feigned ignorance. "What app?"

He ran his hand up the inside of my arm, too quickly for me to pull back before he'd left me feeling as if there were spiders crawling over my skin. I rubbed my arm to ease some of that feeling.

"Hot Guy Hook Ups," he clarified for me.

"What about it?" I was defensive now as I glared up at him. I had a sinking feeling in my gut that I knew where this conversation was going, but I really didn't want to be right.

"How about we come to an arrangement? You take care of me sometimes, and I'll keep your rent the same."

And there went my faith in humanity, all because one douchebag had to be an asshole about it. "No."

But his smile never slipped. "Fine. A few times a week and you won't have to pay rent at all."

I was already tight on money as it was, and I didn't have the extra to be able to move and pay another security deposit plus first and last month's rent. I could ask my friends for help, but none of them were in any better positions than I was. I could ask for more hours, but I knew the rescue didn't have extra money to give me. I could have the hours. That wasn't a problem. There were so many horses to work with and so many house checks to do that if I wanted to work sixty or more hours a week, I could easily do that. But I wouldn't be getting any extra for it.

Having sex with him a few times a week wasn't any more repulsive than having sex with some of the guys I did anyway. I always meant to say no to the ones who were jerks about it or who called me a slut within the first few minutes of meeting me just because I happened to really like sex, but I never did. I had sex with them like I had sex with the nice guys like Grayson who let me come first and never hurt me more than I wanted to be. The awful guys, though, those were the ones I never went back to. I wouldn't have that option here.

15

Could I have sex with this guy without even knowing his name just so that I could keep living in my apartment? Sure. I probably could. But would I like myself at the end of the day? That was another question and one I was afraid of the answer for.

With a sigh I knew I'd made my choice. "You always wear a condom; no one ever knows about this; I don't do any kind of blood, poop, or piss; and you don't get to tie me down. You want to have sex with me, those are my terms."

He laughed. "You want to keep living in this apartment then here are my terms. I get to fuck you at least three times a week. You say someone else's name and it's off, and we're never going out together. I'm not dating you. I just want your ass. And the condom is when I want to use it, not when you do. That clear?"

Like I'd ever be caught dead in public with this asshat. "Sure. But you message me first. On the app. You don't just show up and demand I get naked. I have a job and a life, and this doesn't get to interfere with either of those things."

He didn't seem put out by that at all. "Fine. I'm Brent."

He already knew my name. "Anything else?"

"You working or having that life right now?"

With a sigh I backed up and let him into my apartment. Shit.

Brent closed my door behind himself and snapped his fingers before pointing at the ground like I was some dog for him to boss around. Maybe that's exactly how he thought of me. Was it better to be a slut that wanted this or a whore who couldn't afford rent any other way? I tried not to let those thoughts matter as I took him out of his pants and began giving him the quickest blow job that I could possibly manage.

"Good whore," he moaned as he put his hands in my hair and roughly grabbed me. I went faster, using every trick I knew to get this over with as quickly as possible. He barely gave me any warning before he started coming, but I still managed to pull off of him and he ended up shooting over my chin and chest.

"Thanks," Brent said, putting himself away.

"Yeah." I didn't care that I had come on me when I went to open the door for him. I only wanted him out of my apartment as quickly as possible.

"See you in a few days."

I shrugged. I'd agreed to that, but I wasn't going to give him the impression that I was somehow looking forward to having his dick in my mouth again.

I HEARD from Grayson a few days later. *I'm back in town,* he texted, along with an address. I'd been avoiding going out with everyone else who messaged me, pretty much because I was already feeling degraded enough as it was and didn't need to do it any more, but Grayson was never like that. He gave me the address to a hotel and asked me if I wanted to come join him.

I can be there in an hour, I replied.

I'm looking forward to seeing you again.

I was too. Not just for the sex, but to have someone who didn't call me a whore in the middle of a blow job and who didn't yank on my hair so hard I thought he was going to pull some of it out. I missed being respected, if not cared about, and Grayson gave me that.

I showed up in his hotel room, and he was waiting for me, as usual, but this time he had takeout containers on the little table by the window, and he still had his pants on.

"Hi, Eli. Come, sit down."

"Uh. Hey." I joined him at the table and looked at the various food. Thai, Indian, and Italian. "Couldn't decide?"

He laughed. "I didn't know what you would like. And you said that you don't go out with people, so I thought we could have dinner together in."

Okay, so that was actually a really sweet thought. "Thanks. And, for future reference, the only thing I don't eat is a salad."

Grayson smiled at me, and we began dishing out our various foods onto paper plates. "That is good to know. How've you been?"

I shrugged, and my mind instantly went to my shitty new arrangement with Brent. I wanted to think about the horses, but he was there, his red mottled face above me as he fucked into me and told me, again, what a dirty whore I was as if his insults would start to matter to me at some point.

"You're quiet. Is something wrong?"

I shook my head to get myself out of thinking like that. We didn't talk about each other. Up until last time, I hadn't even known his name. What was I supposed to tell him? I didn't want to break into a friendship zone, but I didn't want to lie to him either. One of the nice things about hooking up with the guys from the app was that I never had to lie to them because there were no expectations of me when we were together. It was just about sex. And now Grayson was messing that up. Still, I had to tell him something. And I felt like I wanted to as well, which was a strange and new experience for me.

"I work at a horse sanctuary, and we had a good week. Lots of adoptions. Yesterday we had an open house with games and stuff." It felt weird, and also kind of good, to tell him even that little bit about myself.

He smiled and gave me a nod. "That's lovely. I pictured you in a counseling center helping people, but helping horses I can also see. I'm a business consultant."

Which sounded like an important and pretty busy job if I had to take a guess. And he'd pictured me in anything? Much less a counseling center? Did that mean that he thought about me in a nonsexual way when we weren't together? My alarms were going off.

"Do you live in Denver?"

We were in the capital now, in the Brown Palace Hotel, which was expensive and old, and taking public transit to get there had been a little tricky. "No. I live—" Shit. I'd been about to tell him what city I lived in. That was a huge nope for me. "I don't live in Denver."

"I don't either. I used to, though. I inherited a house in Thornwood."

I had to stop myself from dropping my forkful of chicken korma back onto the paper plate. I knew someone who lived in Thornwood. Trent, the first guy I'd ever met on the app, was there. I'd been clingy with him, and he'd given me only silence. I'd learned my lesson fast.

"You're wearing glasses today. They make you even cuter, and you look a bit younger with them on."

Was younger better? I wasn't sure, but I liked that he thought I looked cute. "Thanks. I, uh, normally wear contacts." I wanted to stop there, but I realized I was kind of being a jerk when all he was doing was trying to have a conversation with me like two normal people did when they had dinner together. Two normal people who hadn't just learned each other's names after months of having anonymous sex. "I work with a lot of the untrained horses, and sometimes I get thrown, and I've had my glasses break from the fall. Plus they get dirty when I'm riding in the arena when no one has bothered to spray it down to keep the dust from being horrible. So contacts work better for me."

He nodded and finished off his plate of food. He'd brought a ton of it, but he didn't act like it was a big deal either. It was good food, but I was on edge from being surprised with not only dinner but also a conversation with him. Part of me was freaking out, and the other, much saner part of myself was remembering that this was Grayson. I'd known him for months. This was fine, and I wasn't in any kind of danger.

He got up from the table, and I joined him. "If you're not done, you can keep eating. I won't rush you."

"I'm good, thanks." I moved away to begin pulling off my clothes. I knew what came next. This part was familiar to me.

He eased up behind me, and I rested my head on my forearm on the wall. I took out the plug, tossing it aside, and I heard him getting undressed before he put on a condom. Then, instead of fucking me against the wall like he normally would have done, he ran his hands over my lower back.

"You have some scratches. Someone new?"

Great. Of course I did. Fucking Brent. I sighed, probably louder than I meant to. "Something like that."

Maybe he could tell that this was one topic I definitely didn't want to talk about because he dropped it and slid deeply into me without any kind of prep or warning. He was the only one I trusted to be like this with me, because having my body pressed against the wall pretty much made me immobile. I had no leverage if I wanted to get away. But the nice thing about it was that when we were like this, he became all I was aware of. I only saw the wall, and I only felt and heard him. His cologne was faint and reminded me of old woods. And though he fucked me hard, he wasn't rough with me when he touched me. He ran his hands over my body, and he slid his fingers between my legs to cup my balls and hold them as my cock flopped against my stomach with each hard thrust he gave me.

"Eli… Eli… Eli…." He whispered my name, and I closed my eyes. No one knew my name. Maybe it was a mistake to give it to him. Brent never used it, even though he knew it, but the first chance Grayson had, he'd used it. And surprisingly, hearing someone else say my name made my pleasure spike. I whimpered, and I didn't need a dose of quick pain to get me to the edge. All I needed was him pumping away inside of me and his hand on my balls as he kneaded them gently between his fingers even as he roughly took my ass. I cried out and came, and he wasn't long behind me.

Then we stood there shaking and sweaty with him leaning against me and pushing me against the wall as if he needed the balance to be able to stand. He kissed the back of my hair and released my balls only to run his hands over my chest and stomach. He smeared some of my come, but most of it had gone onto the wall or the floor. He didn't seem to care or mind that his hands were getting sticky, though, as he felt me all over as if he was worshipping me. There were no orders for me to get dressed, and no one was there tossing cab money at me as if I was just a few degrees shy of being a rent boy. Instead I had Grayson, who seemed to really care about me on some level. And I began to panic.

"I need you to let me up."

He didn't try to force me to stay. He backed up, and I began getting dressed again. Plug first after washing it, then my jeans, my shirt came next, and then my shoes. I didn't even bother with my socks this time.

"You can stay and shower here," he offered me. Just like he always did.

I was quick to shake my head. This needed to be the last time between us. He couldn't care about me, and I couldn't fall for him. I was a mess, and I was clingy, and I knew what I was good for, and a relationship wasn't it.

"Thanks, but that wouldn't be a good idea. Bye."

I was already halfway out the door when he said, "I'll let you know the next time I'm in town." I didn't say anything back to him after that.

CHAPTER FOUR

Grayson

I TRIED messaging Eli the next day when my trip was canceled at the last minute. But he didn't respond. When I got back from another trip two weeks later, he didn't respond to that message either. I tried a few more times, but after a month of sending him messages, I'd known when to stop. I wasn't going to keep asking him to spend time with me when he had so decisively made things clear to me that he was no longer interested in seeing me. I only wondered what I'd done to deserve the cold shoulder from him. I'd been kind, and I'd been interested in what he had to say. I hadn't pressured him to do anything, ever, and I'd respected every boundary he ever set for us. I just didn't get it.

My next client, surprisingly, was in Parker. I rarely had clients in Colorado. In fact, I couldn't remember the last time I had one, and I loved not having to travel for my latest job. My client was Evaline Green, who was a sweet-sounding older woman who ran a place called the Green Acres Equine Sanctuary. Not surprisingly, she was losing money, as most animal rescues often were. But I had some nonprofit experience, and I wasn't lacking money in the least, especially since I no longer had a mortgage to pay, so I was able to accept the price she offered for my services. Even though it was nearly half of what I would have normally asked for.

As I was driving down from Thornwood to Parker and grumbling at the traffic I was hitting even on a Friday morning, I couldn't help thinking of Eli and how he'd said he worked at a horse rescue. I'd admired him for that, for working with animals and helping them. It was a far cry from what I did, but I thought that it fit what little I'd known of him. Now that he was out of my life, I had no idea what to think of him.

But as I pulled up to a dilapidated wood barn and saw him standing outside with a sanctuary polo shirt on and a clipboard that he held clutched to his chest, my mood brightened instantly.

His eyes widened when I got out of my car, and his cheeks darkened as he looked away.

"Hello," I said as I came up to him.

Eli looked up at me. There were dark smudges under his eyes and a trace of fear in his gaze.

"I'm not going to say anything," I assured him. To prove my point, I extended my hand. "Good morning. I'm Grayson Pendleton. Evaline hired me to go over the financials of the rescue and see how she can squeeze a few more pennies out for the horses."

He gave me his hand, though he was trembling, and I took the lead by shaking his hand before he could pull it out of my grasp. "Eli Walker. I'm a senior employee here, and I handle the adoptions. When Evaline is called out unexpectedly like this, I assist visitors. I can't be around all the time. You'll have to call if you need something. I'll explain all that once we're inside."

He took his hand out of mine as soon as he was done talking. "Please follow me to the office."

The office was little more than a poorly converted stall in the barn. It smelled of hay, leather, and horses, which were all scents I hadn't experienced since I was a child on my grandfather's farm and weren't all that welcome to me now. Still, I had a job to do, so I squared my shoulders and took a seat behind the desk where Eli indicated I sit.

"Does she keep everything on a laptop somewhere?" I asked him once I realized that there was no desktop in front of me.

Eli gave me a sheepish smile. "Um... I do. And I transfer all the documentation to it at the end of the day, but Evaline likes to work with the hard copies." He crouched down at a safe behind me and pulled out a laptop with a bright rainbow pride sticker on it.

"You certainly aren't subtle," I said with some appreciation as he opened the laptop, unlocked it, then turned it around to face me.

"I don't have any reason to be." He moved back, putting some much-needed distance between us. He was working, as was I, but that didn't diminish my body's easy reaction to him in the least. My cock seemed to know no boundaries when it came to him, and I was able to easily picture him on his knees in front of me even here in a horse barn. He pointed to a folder marked Important: For The Rescue before he put a walkie-talkie down beside my hand. "I have one too. We only use one channel here, so be careful what you say over it. If you need some help or can't find something, let me know."

"You aren't staying?" I'd assumed I'd have his help for the day, or at least his company since I likely wouldn't need his help.

He shook his head and moved even farther away. "No. I have stuff to do too. And I'm pretty sure I'd just get in your way. There's a bathroom and a vending machine in the barn here if you need either. See you."

"Eli?" I stopped him.

He turned back to me at the stall's open door. "Yes?"

"I missed you."

He ducked his head to hide his blush. "Use the walkie if you need anything."

"I will," I said, but he was already walking away from me.

A few hours later, he came back to me with a sandwich, a bag of chips, and a soda in his hands. "Everyone is fed lunch here," he explained as he put them on the desk in front of me. His brisk tone made me think he didn't want me thinking he was doing me a favor or treating me any differently than anyone else at the rescue.

"Thank you. Do you have a minute? I have some questions."

He perched himself on the edge of the desk. "Sure. I guess. What's going on?"

I took a deep breath and leaned back in the chair. Truthfully I had no questions about the rescue or its operations. Everything pertaining to Green Acres was well documented and easy to find. Whether that was because Eli kept the files on his computer neat and organized or that was how Evaline insisted they be, I had no idea, and I didn't really care. Her margins were already tight, and I was struggling to find anywhere that could be cut. Perhaps if she didn't insist on feeding everyone while they were there, but I was pretty sure she would have still wanted to thank the volunteers for their time in some fashion.

"Why have you been avoiding me?"

He narrowed his gaze at me and started to slip off the desk, but I grabbed his wrist to stop him. He looked down at my hand on his skin, and I would have given anything to know what he was thinking right then.

"I thought you wanted to talk business," he finally said after a few moments.

"Please?"

With a sigh he came back onto the desk, and I released his hand. "I let you get too close. You were almost in friend territory."

Yes, we had been getting close to friends. But I'd been looking forward to that new development in our dynamic. It seemed that Eli had wanted to be anything but. "And friends is…." I tried to come up with a word that I thought would fit, but nothing came to mind. "Wrong?"

His quick nod left me feeling like he'd slapped me. "Yes. We can't be friends."

"I see."

"I'm glad."

I had been hungry before, but now I had definitely lost my appetite. "Is it my age that prevents you from wanting me as your friend, or is it because I'm black?"

"What? No." He genuinely looked like I'd offended him. He chewed on his lip for a while as I watched him, no idea what was going on in his head. "We can't be friends because when I get to that point, with anyone, I end up getting clingy and needy and inevitably wanting to be with them. So I don't have sex with my friends, and I don't become friends with the people I have sex with."

His brand of logic made no sense to me. I didn't mind the possibility of a relationship with him on the basis of more than sex. But if that's all he was willing to give me, if he even still was, then I knew I'd settle for that in order to have him in my life on any kind of a basis.

I leaned forward over the table to be closer to him. "If we went back to not knowing anything about each other beyond our names, then would you go back to agreeing to meet with me?"

"I've never tried to rewind things before."

"But?"

He gently smiled, but he was no longer looking at me. Instead he was focusing on the wall across from himself. "If you think you can be like that with me, then we can try. I don't want to be friends, though, so you need to remember that."

I wanted to be more than just someone who messaged him for sex and spent an hour or two a week with him, but if that was all he was willing to give me, then I would agree. "I think that will work."

"Thanks for seeing it my way."

If his way was that I'd agreed to continue to treat him like a no-name hookup then sure, that's what I'd do. But I certainly didn't agree with the way he wanted things to be, and I didn't see why he would want that either. We weren't friends, though, and I couldn't force him to accept me in his life as anything more than a casual sex partner.

"Do you want to stay for lunch?" My appetite was back, to a degree, and I would have welcomed his company.

Eli shook his head. "I need to get back to work. I already had my lunch."

To me it sounded suspiciously like he was trying to avoid me again. He must have been able to read some of that on my face because he smiled as if to soften my rejected offer.

"I really do have work to do. We got a mare in last month that has some medical issues and needed a lot of weight put on her. The vet cleared her yesterday for an evaluation, so I get to see if she can be ridden and what she knows. I'm hoping not to get thrown again today."

That was probably the most he'd ever told me about himself or his life, and listening to him, even for such a short amount of time, had me smiling. "You fell off today? Were you hurt?"

He got off the desk. "I'm okay. The arena is soft. And now we know that horse bucks at a canter. The vet will look at him, and then Evaline decides if a trainer needs to come out or if he should be adopted to someone with enough experience to handle a horse with that behavioral issue."

"Adopt him out as is," I told him, even though my opinion wouldn't matter.

"Why? He'd be easier to place after a few months of training."

He was right, but he hadn't been going over the numbers all morning either. "The sanctuary's base price for a rideable horse is five hundred. When that horse is well trained and a child can ride it, that price only goes up to one thousand.

Evaline has spent more money fixing issues like your bucking horse than she will ever make back. But you may say that the money she spends on one horse to get him a home helps other horses down the road, only it doesn't because each horse needs at the very least vet care, farrier care, and hay. In the winter they are given feed and blankets, and during the summer they get extra farrier care. Some of this is offset by donations, but the majority of the income for this sanctuary comes in the form of adoptions, and unless she has a string of free, completely kid-ready, rideable horses come in that need no additional vet or farrier work, other than what each horse gets as a minimum, she cannot keep affording to get these horses trained. So my suggestion to her will be, in order to cut the most costs, that she stop training horses if she wants to keep her sanctuary going for longer than the next two years."

Eli just stared at me for a long time. "How long have you been working with horses?"

I sighed and rubbed the bridge of my nose. I hadn't meant to say all that, but talking business and explaining my choices and my suggestions was easy to me, even when I wasn't speaking to the person who had hired me.

"I don't. I spent a few summers on my grandfather's farm as a kid."

"You picked up a lot. So finding a free trainer is the only solution?"

Nodding, I reached for the soda he'd brought me and opened it. "That would do it, but I've never heard of such a person that would have the knowledge to work with problem horses. You already know that, though. Training a horse from the ground up is one thing. Correcting behaviors is another."

"I'll think about a solution. I would prefer to get these horses trained and then placed into homes where I know they won't be a danger to anyone based on behaviors that we know about."

He could think all he wanted about it, but I was pretty sure we'd both come up with the same answer. The horses needed to be adopted out as-is as long as they were medically treated for any immediate needs. The chronically sick horses were another problem, but even from what little I knew of Evaline, I was pretty sure she wouldn't agree to stop taking those horses in. She seemed to genuinely care about the horses she rescued, and some she'd had on the property for twenty years according to the records Eli had.

"See you," Eli said after a few moments.

I nodded, and he left me alone in the stall to continue my work. Normally I would begin an evaluation by looking at any employees and seeing if there was some overlap of responsibilities there that the employer could restructure and cut down so that one employee might feel overworked for a while until things smoothed out but so that the employer wasn't paying two salaries. The problem with the sanctuary, though, was that there were no employees other than Eli, and he made very little as it was and his position came with no benefits. I wondered how he even managed to survive on such a low income unless he had another job. That was the only option that made sense, but since we weren't going to be friends, I tried not to think about him and his life. I'd get to enjoy sex with him, and that was it. I should have been happy about that instead of feeling like I'd just been on the losing end of a compromise I didn't want to make.

CHAPTER FIVE

Eli

I HADN'T expected Grayson to be able to keep his promise of just sex between us, but when he stopped messaging me just to say hi, I got my hopes up. When he gave me an address and asked me to be there at a specific time, like he'd done in the months before the night I'd let him get too close, I was happy to accept.

Maybe I shouldn't have agreed to go see Grayson, but I really wanted the break from what had essentially become my life of working and screwing Brent with very little in between. It seemed like he was watching me sometimes, waiting for me to come home just so he could text. And I didn't feel comfortable saying no to him. That was the worst part of it. I had this gut feeling that if I ever did refuse, he'd take that as me agreeing to pay rent again, and I couldn't afford to even pay what my rent had been at this point since I'd had some unexpected bills come up. I was in a rut, and I felt trapped. Grayson was definitely a welcome change from the mundane life I'd started to lead without even trying to.

His hotel was in Black Hawk this time, and since I knew he lived in Thornwood now, this hotel couldn't have been more than a ten-minute drive for him. For me it was over an hour, but by the time I got to the casino hotel, I was much more relaxed than I had been when I'd decided to meet up with him. I'd come straight from work too, and instead of changing out of my sanctuary polo shirt, I simply went up to his room in that. I kept a few extra shirts in my car so that no one would ever know where I worked, but with Grayson I didn't have to worry about that. It was a strange sort of situation we found ourselves in, and part of me really wanted it to work out for us just being fuck buddies. The other part of me was ready to swear off guys for a while in general just so I wouldn't have to have Brent on top of me anymore.

Grayson smiled at me when I came into his hotel room. "Hey."

"Hi." I stripped off my clothes quickly, just like I always did, and he moved the sheet aside. Instead of getting on him right away this time, I knelt between his thighs and gently lapped at the head of his cock for a bit. I hadn't been with anyone but Brent lately, and he didn't really inspire me to take my time and linger in the moment at all. But Grayson did. Maybe it was because he didn't rush me or make me feel degraded for agreeing to be with him. He didn't treat me like he owned me and he was somehow allowing me to do him a favor by getting on my knees for him.

So I took my time with Grayson's cock, and I tasted his salt, and I buried my nose in his tight curls when I took him deep into my mouth. And though he whispered my name, he said nothing else to me. I wasn't his whore or his slut. I was just Eli with him, and now he knew a lot more about me than most people I met up with did. Before I could get him too close to coming, I slid over his lap and took out my plug. A condom came next, and then I sank onto him, and he laid his hands gently over my thighs. Riding him was always pleasant, and I used to look forward to the times when I would find him on his back on the bed. Now I practically needed these moments between us.

"You've got some bruises," he said as I began slowly swaying on his cock and worked to find the angle that would be best for me.

Was this part of being friends, or was it a question I could answer? I'd thought he'd meant from when I'd fallen off a horse the day before, but his gaze was on my upper arm, where bruises wrapped around my bicep. Where Brent had been just a bit too rough with me. I didn't know what to tell him. I didn't want to lie, but I didn't want to intentionally cross that barrier either. So I simply shrugged. Grayson lifted one hand off my thigh to be able to trace those dark purple marks on my arm.

"Would you tell me if someone was hurting you? More than you would like them to?"

I shook my head. That was the truth. I wouldn't tell him. Because we weren't friends and I didn't want his help in this situation. I didn't need it either. Brent was foul, and he was a bully, and I hated having sex with him, and I never once got off, and he didn't seem to care in the least, but this was my mess that I'd created, and I was going to live with it until I had enough money to find a new place. Or until I stopped caring about who used my body and how. I was afraid that I was dangerously close to that point already.

"Do you have anyone you could tell?"

I really wished he would drop it. They were just bruises. They didn't matter. I got banged up horseback riding all the time. Just because I now had bruises from sex didn't change the fact that I bruised easily, and he didn't have to worry about me.

"It's not a big deal."

He looked sad, and I realized that I was losing him as he started to go soft inside of me.

"Do you want me to stop?" I went still on top of him.

Grayson moved his hand from my arm, up my neck, to cup my cheek. "No. I want you. I just wish we didn't have limits on our friendship to the point where there wasn't one. Your bruise looks like someone really tried to hurt you, and it makes me worried about you. We're not friends, by your choice, but if you ever did need something, I would help you out."

I shook off his hand and didn't know what else to do. I didn't want to be friends because I didn't want to lose him. I didn't want to fall for him because I didn't want him to see me clingy and needy like I always was when I got into a relationship. But sometimes dealing with Brent made me feel like parts of me were being chipped away. It had only been a bit over a month, but I already felt as if I didn't know how much more of this I could handle. He was just so demanding and impossible, and he treated me like crap all the time and—

Grayson grabbed me and turned me over so that he was on top of me. I pulled my knees up to my chest and waited for him to pound into me like he usually did when he was in this position. I hadn't gotten to come this time, but I was used to not getting to when I was with people now. I didn't expect it from Brent, and maybe Grayson had just gotten tired of me doing nothing, and he decided to take over for the evening. That would make sense to me.

But instead he kissed my cheek and stroked down my sides, to my hips, then to my legs, where he helped wrap them around his waist instead of keeping them pressed against my chest.

"I won't ask you what's going on, Eli. I know, as someone who isn't your friend, it's not my business. But I don't want you to be hurting either. So why don't you tell me what you need from me tonight?" He kissed my neck, and I closed my eyes. I was dirty and tainted from what I'd agreed to with Brent, and I didn't deserve the kindness of this stranger right now.

I licked my lips and started to talk, even though I still had my eyes closed. "Will you be gentle with me tonight?" I'd come there and agreed to meet with him. I had no right to ask him to change what he wanted just for me. But I really needed slow and soft right then. Another round of the kind of sex Brent liked and

I felt like I might break apart. Grayson liked things rough too, but not like Brent did. He wasn't an asshole like Brent, and he didn't make me feel dirty afterward either.

He kissed my lips. "Sure. I've been wanting to make love to you for a while now."

I didn't even know what making love meant, but apparently to Grayson it meant that he'd go slow enough that I felt every thick inch of him as he stroked into me. It meant his hair would rub against my smooth skin and that he would softly kiss me every second he could. He touched me all over, and he was gentle every single time. When he spoke it was only to say my name or to tell me how good I felt under him or to say that I was beautiful. He grunted and gasped as he lost his words, and yet, before he came, he wrapped his hand around my cock and stroked me until I found my own orgasm. Only then did he come.

This time when he was done, he didn't simply roll off of me. He moved away from me, sure, but it was only to toss the condom in the trash, then move me on my side so that he could come up behind me. He didn't try to put his dick in me again or mess with me at all while he had me there. Instead he just wrapped his arm around me and slid his other under my head to give me a bit more of a pillow.

I was frozen there. I didn't do this with anyone. Not since I'd tried and been turned down so harshly. I didn't even like thinking about my first time because to him I'd been just another screw, and to me I'd practically been in love with him because I'd been naive and stupid and thought a few messages on a damn hookup app somehow made us in a relationship. He'd been nice to me up until I'd wanted to see him again. And I'd wanted to lie just like this with him too. Being with Grayson like that made me think of my first guy. He hadn't even known he'd been my first. And Trent had been such a fucking ass about it too. Not returning my messages at all.

"Do you want to talk about it?" Grayson asked me.

"About what?"

He tightened his arm around me, pulling me in even closer against him to the point where I was surprised he was even able to breathe. "I'd like to know why you were so upset. But I also don't want you to shut me out again. So I'll leave that up to you."

I closed my eyes and tried to decide what to do as he let his fingers roam over my stomach. I didn't have a good answer, though. "I made a mistake, and now I'm kind of trapped doing something I really don't want to do. But I felt like I didn't have a choice at the time."

"And now you do?"

I wish I did. I would love to tell Brent to fuck off the next time he texted me to come over. But no, I didn't get to do that. I couldn't even really think about it because every time I did, I ended up just getting angry at him and even more so at myself for being so stupid. I could have worked less and taken a second job instead of accepting his deal. I could still do that. But the damage to my pride was already done. And part of me didn't even care anymore.

"Not really," I quietly admitted.

He moved his hand from my stomach up to my chest, and I lay there limp beside him as I became more and more miserable.

"Tell me what I can do to help."

I shook my head and looked over at the open blinds. The sheer curtains were still drawn, and the bright lights of our own little mountain version of Las Vegas flickered beyond them.

"Little hard to tell you how to help me when I don't even want to tell you the problem."

I needed to go. Staying there in his arms would just make me more miserable than I already was. I started sliding away from him, and he let me go a little more easily than I would have liked. I wanted to argue with him about how I couldn't stay and how we weren't friends. But he didn't say anything as I climbed off the bed and got dressed. Once I did look back at him, I wished I hadn't. There was so much pity in his eyes. I instantly looked away.

"Do I get to see you again?" he asked.

I shrugged. I didn't know right now. This was all such a mess. "Do you think you want to?"

I heard him get off the bed, but I didn't turn back to look at him. He came up behind me and hugged me tightly. I felt like a little more of me was chipping away. "I do. You're my favorite part of being in Colorado."

I shouldn't have smiled at such a sentimental thing to say. But I did. "Thank you," I whispered.

He kissed the back of my head and let me go. I headed home a few minutes later.

CHAPTER SIX

Grayson

WHATEVER WAS bothering Eli also got to me over the next two weeks I spent in Miami. I was in the middle of sun-scorched beaches and men who thought a bit of string and spandex constituted a bathing suit. I should have been in heaven. Instead I couldn't stop thinking about Eli and the sadness that he'd worn like a second skin the last time I'd seen him. For months he'd been so full of life and so easy to smile. Then, somewhere, something had gone wrong. I couldn't shake these thoughts of him while I worked or had someone else in my bed. I didn't say Eli's name while I was with them, thankfully, but it was a close thing.

By the time I got back to Colorado, I was ready to get some answers out of him, as long as he was willing to give them to me. I messaged him as soon as I was off the plane. *I'm back in Colorado. Can I see you tonight?*

He replied back within ten minutes. *Wish I could. But I'm busy.*

I should have left it alone, but I didn't. I should have kept my mouth shut. But after two weeks of obsessing over him, I needed answers. *Busy with the person who bruised your arm?* I asked him. I didn't expect an answer, but I got one anyway. And it was almost immediate.

Yes. Sucks. See you tomorrow?

I wanted to tell him to blow this guy off, to tell him not to go through with whatever he was doing that was so terrible. But

I was afraid of saying anything because I didn't want him to run again. I'd lost him once by trying to get close to him, and I was determined not to do that again. Not to either of us. So I held back what I wanted to say and instead just sent him a message saying, *Sure*. I reserved a room at a hotel, sent him the address, and told him to come over whenever.

I didn't have any plans. I rarely did once I was off work. That was the beauty of not having to work while I was in Colorado. Usually. Evaline Green wanted to do a phone follow-up when I had a chance, so I'd likely do that in the morning, but otherwise I was free to go to my favorite restaurants and meet up with my friends.

That night I met with my closest friend at a restaurant a few blocks away from his condo in downtown Denver. He lived on the twentieth floor and faced the city. Nigel Coleman was two years older than me, which put him right at fifty, and his heritage was a mix of black, Mexican, and Native American. I'd thought he was attractive, once, but not anymore. Too many cigars had tainted my desire for him as anything more than my friend.

We shook hands as we met in front of Singing Blackbird, a brand-new restaurant the local magazines had apparently given rave reviews. Getting a table was supposed to be hard to do, but Nigel knew people. He greased palms and offered smiles where needed. Otherwise he was perfectly fine looking down at everyone else around him, all in their perfect little places. As long as they were beneath him.

"I see you're still on that phone app," Nigel said as we were seated.

I'd seen the menu online. I already knew I was going to be having the roasted duck breast with a glass of merlot. "I am. I still enjoy male company whenever I can get it."

"As long as you're protecting yourself."

I smiled at him and was glad when a waiter came over to take my drink order. I adored Nigel, most of the time, but he was much easier to deal with after I'd had a glass of wine. Or two. Especially when he decided to get self-righteous with anything that had to do with my life.

"I am. And I've been seeing someone from the app regularly. His name is Eli."

Our drinks came, and Nigel sipped his wine, as did I. "What does he do for work?"

"He works with animals."

That got his nod of approval. "A veterinarian. Well, at least he does something with his life, unlike most of the world."

I didn't correct Nigel's assumption. He would never need to meet Eli, so there was no reason to begin an argument. But then I realized there was no reason not to tell Nigel just who Eli was anyway. They would never be meeting, but what did I care what Nigel thought of someone I was regularly having sex with? The easy answer was I didn't.

"Actually, he works at a horse rescue. He's sort of an everything man, from what I can tell. And according to his boss, he does his job well."

Nigel scoffed and lifted his chin a little higher. "Typical. Just once I'd like to see you spending time with someone who deserves you instead of these bits of rough that you like to play with."

I laughed and nearly snorted my wine in the process. I had to put it down before I spilled it over the white linen tablecloth. "Nigel, I'm having sex with him, not marrying him. You can relax. How is your sex life going?"

"Same old same old, I guess. When I find a man worth spending time with, then I do so."

I thought his bed must be pretty cold, then, since so few people qualified. But I didn't say that. "Sounds lovely."

"What are you doing tonight?"

It had been a long time since he'd given me such a blatant invitation. And I really wasn't interested in taking him up on his offer either. "I've got plans."

"The horse boy?" Nigel guessed incorrectly.

I just smiled at him. I wished I was meeting up with Eli tonight, but that wasn't going to be happening until tomorrow night. I did worry about him, though. If Nigel was a police officer, or anything even remotely helpful for me, I might have asked his opinion of what Eli was going through, from what little I knew. But Nigel was an investment banker. He was good with money, but not much else. And he liked to buy antiques. His condo was filled with them. He knew a good deal about each of them too, and if we were in his condo now, I was sure I would get an earful about some small fragment of pottery from a civilization thousands of years old.

We spent a few hours there, but by my third glass of wine, I was glad to go home. Until I actually got through my front door. My house was big and in the mountains. Every room had a decent view. It should not have felt as cold and uninviting as it did. But as soon as I entered, I had to force myself to stay and not turn right back around and go book a hotel room. I could have afforded it, and I'd chosen to stay in hotels instead of in the house before, but it seemed like a ridiculous thing to do when I had a house there just standing empty for me. When I wanted to use it.

The next afternoon I ignored the fact that I had reservations at a hotel and sent Eli my home address. I'd debated doing it for a long time, but in the end I decided I wanted him there. I hadn't brought anyone to my home before, but I was tired of having Eli in hotels, and the last time I'd been with him had sealed the deal for me. I didn't care about anyone else I was with except for him. And I couldn't get his look of sadness out of my mind.

That's the address to your house. Isn't it? Eli messaged me only seconds after I'd sent it to him.

Yes. No use trying to play games with him when I wanted him there with me as soon as he could possibly manage to get up to Thornwood.

He waited nearly twenty minutes to message me again. *Okay. I'll be there soon.*

I could hardly contain my surprise. Or my excitement. *Great. I'm looking forward to seeing you again.*

Me too. His last message made me smile down at my phone, and I decided that I needed to walk over to the only grocery store in town to get us a bottle of red wine and the nicest box of chocolates Thornwood had to offer, which still wasn't all that great. I felt like pampering him to reward him for agreeing to come up to my house.

There was a sign in the window of the diner that said they had fresh chocolate chip cookies, so I stopped there and picked up four. I wasn't into milk and cookies anymore, not since my teens, but a few to snack on wouldn't go amiss, I didn't think.

When I opened my front door for Eli a short time later, I handed him a glass of wine, and by his look of apprehension when he sniffed it, I realized he either didn't drink, or really didn't like wine. Maybe he was more of a beer person. I supposed that I should have asked him instead of simply assuming he would enjoy the same vintage I did.

"Thank you for coming over," I said as I closed the door behind him.

"I haven't been to a guy's house before from the app. Or at all actually. If you were running out of money for expensive hotel rooms, we could have screwed in the back of a car. I've done that plenty of times, and I don't mind."

I hated the thought of him being treated that casually, or of expecting me to do the same to him. "I haven't had sex in a car since I was seventeen, and I'm not about to start again now. The reason I asked you to come here tonight, though, was because I wanted to spend time with you, beyond having sex with you."

He eyed me cautiously. "Why?"

I laughed without meaning to and led him over to my couch so that we were no longer standing in front of my door. "Because I like spending time with you."

He looked at me as if I wasn't making any sense. "Usually all we ever do is screw." He sipped his wine.

I crossed one leg over my knee and tried to think of a decent response that would explain to him that I enjoyed those moments where I'd held him very much. But he kept playing with the collar of his turtleneck as if it was annoying him. It wasn't cold enough out to require him to wear one, so I reached over and pulled his collar down, both dreading and expecting what I was sure I was going to see there. When I caught sight of the three dark bruises over his throat, I sighed and released him. I found Eli looking at me as I leaned back against my couch and stared into my glass of wine.

"Say something," he urged me.

"Is he your boyfriend?" That was the only thing I could think of to ask him.

But Eli just chuckled and put his glass of wine down on the coffee table. I was so upset that I didn't even reach for a coaster to protect the dark wood. "I don't have one of those. I never have."

I was so surprised by his revelation that I was momentarily distracted from his bruises. "But you must have dated someone at some point in your life." I fully understood, and embraced, sex for pleasure without the attachment and complication of a relationship. But I'd still dated men, especially when I was younger and thought there was a chance of finding that special person my friends all insisted was out there for me. I'd grown up and given up that impossible idea of a soul mate long ago, but Eli was far too young to have come to that same conclusion so soon.

Eli pulled one of his legs under him, the other he brought up to his chin. "No, I haven't. I'm sure you think it's weird, but as soon as I was out of my parents' house, and therefore able to be myself and date who I wanted to, which was every cute guy I could find, I was on the app, and that's not for dating."

I didn't know what to say. I could connect the dots, and I assumed I knew what he was saying. But I didn't want to think of a young, or at least younger since he was hardly old by anyone's standards, Eli losing his virginity to someone on Hot Guy Hook Ups. I knew how I'd treated him and how most people probably treated each other on the app. It was for anonymous sex at a moment's notice, not for dating and definitely not for falling in love.

"Did you put so little value on your virginity?" I asked.

He looked away from me, but only long enough to pick up his glass of wine and take a sip of it. He made a face, like he really didn't like the taste of it, then put it back down. "I didn't, but I was too nervous, and I forgot to get his name, and after it was done, I tried texting him, and he refused to respond. I learned pretty quickly what kind of value guys put on each other within the app. And, judging from the times I've been to the clubs in Denver, things aren't that much different out in the world either."

"No, they aren't. If you let people treat you like all you're good for is sex, people generally will. It's rare that anyone will give you any kind of push back against that."

"You didn't, not at first anyway."

He didn't sound angry about that at all. He was simply stating a fact like it was currently dark outside, which it was. But I didn't like that about myself at all. And I hated that he'd realized that and pointed it out. I didn't mean to be like that with him, and I would have loved to have known his name before I did, but I hadn't insisted on it. Maybe I should have. But he'd been so secretive whenever I'd asked him any questions about himself that I was afraid I would have lost him completely. "I'm sorry. I should have tried harder to get answers out of you from the beginning. I always wanted to know about you. Ever since the start."

He blushed a little. "I wouldn't have answered you. I still don't want you knowing things, so don't think this is going to be some big turning point. I'm just feeling a bit more relaxed right now. Probably since you've seen me at my job, and now you know me with my clothes on." He shrugged, and I decided to move on to what I really wanted to know.

"Do you like being hurt?" I quietly asked him.

He'd been playing with his collar again, off and on, but stopped as soon as I finished asking my question. "Not anything more than what you do for me when we're together. Pinching my nipples or something like that. It works for me."

"But trying to strangle you doesn't?" I needed that clarified. If there was something I could try to give him to satisfy that need of his, then…. No. I couldn't even begin to imagine putting my hands around his throat, much less enjoying it.

"No. It doesn't. Can we talk about something else?"

His tone told me he would rather talk about anything but the bruises around his throat. But I wasn't done with that line of questioning yet. "When I'm done finding out what you're doing in such a dangerous situation." He started to get up, but I grabbed his hand. I wasn't going to trap him there and force him to tell me, but I didn't want him to run away from me either just because I wanted to know that he was safe. "Please stay."

"I won't tell you what's going on."

I expected that. I'd pushed him too far, too fast. I wanted to know what was going on with him, but I wasn't going to risk losing him either. "Stay. I won't ask you about what you're going through again or why you'd put up with someone hurting you like you are."

Eli sighed and went back to sitting down next to me. I thought that would be the end of it, but then he spoke again. "I'm trading sex with him for something I need. That's all it is."

"Drugs?" I immediately guessed. But Eli just rolled his eyes. "Then what?"

"Do you want in my ass tonight?" he asked me bluntly, and I knew where he was going with that question. I needed to not ask him any more questions if I wanted him to stay with me longer than the next five minutes.

"I want you to stay," I replied. I didn't absolutely need to have him in my bed that night, but I wouldn't have turned him down either. Instead I wanted his company, and to get that from him, I was willing to stop asking him so many questions he clearly wasn't interested in and were possibly making him uncomfortable too.

He smiled at me and started stripping off his shirt. "Then let's go. Where do you want me?"

He was always so beautiful to me. His pale skin, his lack of hair, his bright pink nipples, his subtle muscles that I now knew were likely from years of working with horses. At one time I'd thought he'd been a dancer. Something classical like ballet and in a company in Denver. There'd been a time, months ago, that I'd had dreams of going to see him perform, bringing him a bouquet of luscious red roses at the end of his performance, and having him kiss me in front of the whole audience.

But with his shirt off, I couldn't stop staring at his neck. Until he sighed. "Figure it out, Grayson. Either you want me, despite my neck, or you're going to stare at those marks the whole time we're together, which, in that case, won't be very long. They don't bother me. I'm over it. But I need you to snap out of it if you expect me to stay here right now."

He was right. So I tried not to think about someone putting their hands around his neck and squeezing his skin hard enough to make him bruise. And I forced myself not to picture Eli lying there, taking that kind of torture, in trade for whatever he thought he needed. It was too much and even as I tried to stand up and take him back to my bedroom, where I would have laid him down and been inside of him, much like I was picturing someone else doing while they tried to strangle him, I couldn't.

I shook my head and sat back down on the couch. "Maybe you should just go." I took a long drink of my wine and wished I could change things for him, whatever his circumstances were.

He hesitated. "Because the bruises bother you that much? I can keep my shirt on if you want. If it'll help."

I thought Eli was sweet to offer the compromise, since I knew how much he hated wearing anything while he was having sex. But the bruises weren't what I had a direct issue with.

"They aren't the problem," I said as I leaned back and looked up at him while he stood there above me. "I keep imagining someone doing that to you, and I can't help feeling disgusted by the whole human race at the idea of someone wanting to hurt you for what I can only assume was their own sick amusement. I can't help but picture you lying under someone while they have their hands around your throat, and for whatever reason, you allow it to happen."

He came over and knelt on the couch beside me. I took his hand when he offered it to me. "I won't come over when I have bruises again."

"I'd rather that you not be in a position where you're being bruised. You've had marks on your body this time and last time.

If this continues and you decide not to subject me to your bruised body, I may never see you again."

Eli looked away from me, and I realized he had no idea when this situation, whatever it was, would stop. Did he owe this person for the next month? Or was he trapped in whatever he was doing for a year or more?

"Will you please tell me what's going on? Maybe I could help you." I was practically pleading with him, and I wasn't above begging him.

Eli shook his head, and he wouldn't look back up at me. Instead he slid from the couch to the floor and began undoing my pants. I put my hands over his, but he was insistent.

"Please?" He'd already taken my soft cock out.

I lay back and closed my eyes, giving him permission. If he didn't want to talk about it, I wouldn't be able to make him. But maybe he'd let me give him pleasure. I doubted that he got that with whoever he was with who liked to hurt him, and I knew from the app that he hadn't been active on there recently, except to talk to me.

"Back on the couch, pants off," I told him softly. The words might have been a command, but I made sure my tone didn't imply that. While he was getting comfortable, I got undressed as well. I knew he liked giving head, so I didn't fight him on that at all. But I didn't force him down or become rough with him either. There were times that I had. I'd even fucked his mouth while he was leaning back against a wall and I'd stood over him before. That had been rough and beautiful, and we'd both been panting and sated afterward. But tonight I didn't want to be rough with him at all. I simply wanted to touch him and enjoy him as we gave each other pleasure. So I ran my hand through his soft hair, being careful that I didn't tug on the strands at all. With my other hand, I stroked down his back until I ran my fingers into the slit of his ass.

He had his plug in, like he always did. I'd never met someone who was comfortable wearing one for as long as Eli did. It was as if the toy had become just another piece of clothing to him. He hadn't removed it for me this time, as if he knew I didn't intend to be inside of him that night. I couldn't be over him while I was thinking about someone else having violent sex with him. I pushed on his plug, and he pressed himself into the cushions of my black leather couch while also putting his mouth back over me. I was getting harder now at the sight of his perfectly round ass, even before I felt the slickness of his tongue against my head. He had a wonderful mouth, but it was the soft sounds that he made while he was giving me pleasure that really worked in my favor. He sucked me like he enjoyed it too, and not like it was a chore for him to go through before he could get to something better, or before he was done with me. I'd been with enough men in my lifetime to know the difference between someone who was simply going through the motions when it came to sucking someone off and someone like Eli who seemed to genuinely enjoy the experience.

As he gave my cock his attention, I played with the plug, pushing on it and moving it until he was squirming under my hand and practically humping my couch. It wouldn't take much longer now. I'd been with him enough times to know the signs of when he was close to finding his own pleasure. I got up on my knees to both give him better access to me and also so that I could stroke my hands down his spine as he slid himself against my couch. I loved watching him come, and listening to him was like being at the symphony as each of his soft cries built on the other until it was all a beautiful melody of pleasure and abandon.

He pulled his mouth off of me, and I leaned back so I could see his face. "Is something wrong?"

"I'm close." His cheeks were dark red, and his eyes were full of lust and pleasure. Even if I didn't know his cries, I would have been able to tell that he was close just from looking at his face.

"I know. Go ahead."

He hesitated. "I'll make your couch dirty."

"It's leather. It wipes off easily," I said with a laugh. He smiled and took me back into his mouth, and I placed my palm flat against his plug as I toyed with it inside of him. He arched back on occasion, letting me know he'd liked what I was doing to him. I wanted something that I could stroke into him, but that would have to wait for another time since I didn't own any toys of my own. I imaged that he did, though. Someone who walked around with a plug in his ass all day surely had a collection of toys he could use to fuck himself with when the need arose.

It didn't take long before his humping of my couch became erratic and his cries became hoarser as he got even closer. I knew what would push him over the edge. A bit of pain always worked for him. But in the end, I couldn't bring myself to scratch my fingers over his ass like I'd done before to get him to climax. I pulled on his hair, giving him a light tug and not nearly what I normally would have done, but it seemed to be enough for him, as he moaned around my cock and afterward lay still.

He hadn't stopped using his mouth, though, and his pleasure had brought me close enough to mine that I had to pull back before I came in his mouth. Despite how good he felt in that moment, I was sure he wouldn't have appreciated that slip up from me. So I pulled myself out of his mouth, despite his quiet protests. He turned over as if knowing what was going on, despite his postsex haze, and I stroked myself until I shot long lines of come over his chest and stomach.

Before he could protest, as he always did when I told him he could shower in whatever hotel room I'd booked for us, I had my hand around his wrist and I had brought him to his feet. He resisted, lightly, by dragging his feet, but I wasn't having any of it as I took him to the downstairs bathroom and helped him under the spray of the hot shower. I kept both bathrooms well stocked with my favorite soaps and shampoos, and getting him clean could have been an easy job of simply washing him off like an old gardening bucket.

But once I had him under the spray of the shower, I wanted to linger there with him. He leaned back against the tile and let me wash him. I took my time soaping him up and cupping the water over his skin. He closed his eyes and let me do what I wanted to him. He didn't even lift his arm to protest against me once. And that, by far, was the saddest part of it all, because I could see so easily how someone would take advantage of him in this or any situation. I knew, as well, that I was to blame for this too. Whenever we'd gotten together, he'd been able to come, and I'd always made sure it was first and that I'd never hurt him. I'd made sure that he was okay when he left. But I'd never asked him to meet me just to be able to lavish pleasure on him with no regard for myself. We'd been hooking up for months and maybe that wasn't to be expected of two people in our situation, but it hadn't been so long since I'd dated someone else that I didn't remember what it was like to give pleasure without any expectation of my own being met.

I turned off the water and held Eli close. Getting him dry was no harder for me than it had been to wash him. He was silent and pliant in my hands, even as I finished taking care of him and brought him back to the living room. There he dressed himself as I silently watched.

"Will you stay here tonight?" I hoped he would, even though I knew what his answer was likely going to be.

Eli shook his head, as I expected, and he finished getting his shoes on. "I have an early day tomorrow."

"If something happens and you need a place to be, you're welcome to come here," I told him.

He gave me a long look, then shook his head again. "I have my own apartment."

I was sure that he did, even though we'd never talked about it. He seemed too independent, too unwilling to accept even the slightest bit of help from me, that I couldn't see him living with someone where he'd have to rely on them all the time.

"Will you tell me what's going on with you?"

"No." Eli's snappish tone told me that there would be no discussion on that point. I relented and nodded, conceding to him.

"When you leave here, are you safe?" I pressed him.

Eli sighed and ran his hands through his hair. He messed up the strands, but instead of making his hair look unruly, he only looked like he'd been having fun. Not necessarily like he'd just come, but he had a satisfied look about him. Except when I looked at his eyes. Only then could I really see just how upset he was.

"I'll stop," I said, hating the way he smiled at that, like he was relieved by me giving up.

"No, you won't. But that's because you care for some reason. See you later." He let himself out of my house, and still naked, I pulled the sheer front curtains aside to be able to watch him get into his car, which was at least ten years old and looked completely shabby next to my luxury model. But Eli didn't even give my car a second glance. He'd never known that the car was mine before, since I'd always parked near other cars at any of the hotels we'd been at together, but now that he had to know, he acted like he couldn't have cared less. It was a curious thing. I expected him to react somehow to our obvious difference in wealth. But he just looked up at me and gave me a weary smile as he backed out of my driveway.

CHAPTER SEVEN

Eli

WHEN I got home, I wanted to strip off all my clothes, dump them somewhere in the vicinity of my horribly overflowing laundry basket, and go right to bed. Thanks to Grayson, I didn't need to shower, but I definitely wasn't ready to do anything else that day. And I sure as hell wasn't in the mood. So, when I'd barely been able to get my shirt off and someone came knocking at my door, I had to resist the urge to yell at them. I had to really bite my tongue when I saw Brent on the other side of my door.

"You're supposed to text first," I grumbled at him. "You can't just come over and expect me to put out."

Brent laughed at me and pushed his way into my apartment. Over a month of dealing with him, and I was too tired to fight back, or even argue, at this point. "Yes, I can. And we both know it."

I hoped that I could just get this over with as quickly as possible so that I could take another shower and go back to my day. "Fine. Whatever. What do you want?"

He stepped forward and cupped me through my jeans. I didn't react, and I wasn't ever hard with him. He got bored quickly and went to something he knew would get a reaction from me—yanking on my hair. I cringed, but I didn't cry out this time. I hadn't in weeks.

"You're boring me, Eli."

"Sorry." I wasn't. "What do you want?" I hated having to repeat myself to him. If someone at the rescue didn't understand something right away, I had no problem talking to them for hours about something that had to do with horses, especially when it came to their safety. But Brent could go fuck off for all I cared.

"You, ass up."

I rolled my eyes. "Fine."

"But first I want to see how well you can take a hit." I'd barely heard him, and didn't even have time to register what he was saying, before he punched me in my cheek. I went down, holding my cheek.

At least the rest of the night went quickly.

THE NEXT morning at work, everyone was staring at me. And I didn't blame them one bit. I had a swollen cheek, a split lip, and a black eye. All of my face hurt, and that wasn't even the start of it. Wearing a turtleneck helped, some, but it didn't help with the pain I was in. I'd gone to the clinic after Brent had left, and made up some lie about being mugged. I was relatively sure the police officers there hadn't bought my story, but they hadn't exactly pressed me for more answers either. It was a good thing I wouldn't be seeing Grayson that evening, because he wouldn't have settled for the half-assed answers I'd been able to come up with the night before.

One of my only friends, Mason, came out of the barn and ran when he saw me pull up to the sanctuary. "Holy shit." He hugged me, and I forced myself not to wince too badly. He was twenty-one and absolutely adorable with sun-bleached blond hair. He'd never had a boyfriend and, as far as I knew, was still a virgin. He was so innocent and fragile, and I was sure he didn't even have a place to start from in understanding what I was doing or what I was willingly putting myself through with Brent. So I kept my mouth shut when I could have told him everything.

"What happened to you?" Mason asked me as we headed into the office.

I shrugged like it wasn't a big deal that the guy that I was bargaining my body with had used me as a punching bag too. "Nothing much. Just got mugged. It happens all the time in Denver." It really didn't. And I hadn't even been in Denver last night except to drive down I-25 after getting off 6th Avenue.

"Fuck. Do the police have any suspects? Tell me they arrested someone."

He was adorable and so damn naive. "They're working on it." Lying to him sucked. I knew he looked up to me, which was a stupid thing for him to do, and before Brent had come along, I'd always tried to stand up to whatever ideals he had for me. But now I felt like I was living a lie and any of the community service guys would have been a better role model for him. At least they were honest, generally, about their sins. I was still trying to pretend that Brent didn't even exist most of the time. It had been easier before he started giving me all of the bruises. Back then I could only pretend he didn't exist if I couldn't feel the pain he'd left me in. Now I didn't have that luxury.

I opened the door to the office and froze as I caught sight of Grayson sitting behind Evaline's desk. He looked up at me and frowned, and then his attention shifted over to Mason.

I hugged my best friend again. "I'll see you later."

Mason headed away. As soon as he was gone, I closed the door.

"He's not the one who's doing this," I told Grayson before he could start asking questions or go confront Mason.

But Grayson shook his head. "I didn't think he was. He doesn't look nearly strong enough for the marks on you." He got up from the behind the desk and came over to touch my cheek. I pulled away before he could get too close to me. "I want you to stay with me tonight."

I rolled my eyes and took a seat across the desk from where he'd been sitting. "I'm not really in decent shape for sex today, if that's what you're looking for. Now, why are you here? Again?"

He sat down again in the chair across the desk from me, and I leaned back in my chair. I was so freaking sore and tired. Brent had been done with me quickly, but that didn't diminish what had been done in the least, and a big part of me just wanted it to end. I was seriously considering homelessness at this point, at least for a little while until I was able to get a few more checks in the bank to afford first and last month's rents plus a deposit on a new place, like every apartment I'd contacted was asking. My credit wasn't great, but it wasn't horrible either. The up-front money was the part I was struggling with.

"I'll tell you why I'm here if you tell me why you're going through whatever it is that you're doing."

I sighed as I stared up at the ceiling. Really, what did it matter at all if Grayson thought I was a stupid fucking whore as Brent liked to call me while he was screwing me? Or beating me as he'd done the night before? It didn't matter, but I still couldn't look at him as I confessed my sins to him.

"My rent was increased, and I couldn't pay it, so I took the option that let me not have to pay rent at all."

"I see."

There was no pity or condemnation in his voice. Only a quiet acceptance of my current reality

"So why are you here?" I asked.

"Because Evaline wanted me to go over more figures now that she's moved some of the more medically care-intensive horses into foster homes. She's on her way to an auction right now, and she wants to know how many horses she can bring in. I'm not her accountant and I have no desire to be, but I agreed to help her one more time."

I turned my head to smile at him. "She loves the horses."

"Yes, I'm sure she does." He closed his laptop so that it was no longer between us. "I have an offer for you, one that I hope you fully consider before giving me an answer."

I frowned over at him, but he definitely had my full attention now. Not that he didn't before, of course, but now he wanted something from me.

"I'm listening," I told him.

"My house in Thornwood is nice, but it isn't a home by any means. I inherited it from my father, and I'm rarely there. I didn't even exactly like him, but I suppose having a house is a good thing. I'd like you to take care of it for me."

"Meaning what? Exactly?"

He settled his weight in his chair, and the old plastic shifted with his movement. "I'd like you to consider coming to live with me. You'd only have to keep the house clean and—"

I interrupted him as I tried to bite back on my anger. "And be your live-in fuck toy, right? No thanks. My situation may suck ass, but at least I have my own place."

Grayson was quick to shake his head. "No, I'm not saying that at all. If we want to have sex, that's something that I believe we've both enjoyed in the past. But I'm not asking you to trade your body for a place to live."

I flinched, even though I'd tried not to, because that's exactly what I'd been doing, and I absolutely hated it. But give up my apartment to live in his house? It was better than being homeless. But I didn't know if that was really the answer. I didn't like living with other people, and I didn't know Grayson well enough that I felt that I could trust him.

"How often are you in town?"

He shrugged, but he did smile at me as if he was glad that I was giving his offer even the little chance that I was. "Maybe ten days a month, total. I leave again tomorrow morning, actually, so if you came over tonight, you could try it out, spend the night in your own room, and then you'd have the house to yourself for the next three days to try it out. As long as you keep the house neat and don't break anything, I'd welcome your company while I'm in town, and while I'm away on business, I'll know that the house is being taken care of, which will be a relief for me. Will you at least think about it?"

I stopped leaning back in my chair. "Sure. On a trial period."

"Of course."

He looked happy with my decision, but I wasn't done speaking yet. "You don't own me. I'm not your personal sex toy, and if I want to meet up with someone else, even while you're there, you don't get to decide that for me."

Grayson's smile lost some of its brilliance, but he nodded anyway, agreeing with my demands. "If there's nothing else that you need right now, then I'll make you an extra key this afternoon, and you can bring your things over tonight after you're done with work."

Not so fast. "I'll bring over enough to get me through the night," I countered him.

Grayson leaned across the desk toward me. "I don't think it's a good idea for you to go back to your apartment. It's not safe for you there."

That was an understatement, but he wasn't going to win this round with me. "I'm not bringing all of my stuff over to your house with only a vague idea that I might like living with you. Give me a few days to get used to it, and then we'll see."

But he didn't look convinced. "I only want you to be safe, Eli. Don't be so stubborn about your own well-being. We'll be roommates. I won't expect anything more from you. Have dinner with me sometimes, watch the news with me on the nights I'm at home if you want to. And you'd be welcome in my bed whenever you wanted to be there. But I'm not going to allow you to purposefully endanger yourself simply because you're being too bullheaded to see the merits of coming to live with me."

He'd pushed me to the edge of what I was willing to put up with from him right then. I was being bullheaded? Right.... "Have fun working," I said as I got up from the chair. I was done. I needed my independence, and I wasn't prepared to sign my life and my home over to him when I didn't even know if we could get through a night of living together yet.

Grayson grabbed my wrist, and I looked down at his hand on my skin before I frowned over at him.

"Eli...." He released me and sat back down. "I'm worried about you. But I'm not willing to risk losing you either. I care about you too much. So, fine, just a few things tonight, then."

I rubbed my skin nervously where he'd grabbed me. He hadn't hurt me at all. His touch had been too light for that. But it was a nervous gesture while I was thinking.

"You shouldn't care about me, you know."

He looked completely confused. "And why is that?"

I was already halfway out the door when I turned back to look at him. "Because I'm not worth it. Tonight, then?"

He simply nodded, and I went on with my day without ever signing into work like I'd meant to do when I first came into the office.

CHAPTER EIGHT

Grayson

ELI SHOWED up on my doorstep at just after six. "Hello." I stepped back to let him into the house. He'd only brought his backpack with him, but at least it looked full.

"Hi." He swallowed nervously.

I tried to think of what he would need first. Not dinner probably. Or a glass of wine, not that I wasn't already sipping on some moscato. "I'll show you to your room, and you can put your things down there."

Eli gave me a tentative little smile, and I knew then that I'd made the right choice in where to take him first in my house. I led him upstairs, where there were three rooms. A bedroom on each side of the hall and a bathroom we'd share. It was the master bath, and I had direct access to it from my room, but he'd have to go through the hall. It was better than asking him to use the downstairs one where I'd showered with him before.

"That will be your bedroom, this is the bathroom, and my bedroom is through that door, should you ever want to join me." I looked over at him to gauge his reaction as he opened the door and went inside. There wasn't much there to look at, a bed, a dresser, walls I'd had painted a pale, sunny yellow, back when I'd thought I'd ever have a use for the room as an office. He would have a good size walk-in closet, should he choose to use it.

As I silently watched him, Eli went over and put his backpack down on the bed, which jumped a little under the sudden weight.

The comforter was a dark tan. The catalog called the color coyote. I didn't much care for it myself, but it went with the walls and didn't clash with the dark hardwood floor.

"If you need anything else, I'll get it for you," I promised him. I was still waiting for his reaction to the space I was giving him.

Eli looked at me over his shoulder and gave me a shrug. "Sure. Thanks. But I think this will be fine. Assuming I choose to stay, which wouldn't be more than a month at the absolute most, would I be allowed to put up pictures as long as I use the sticky back stuff and not nails or thumbtacks?"

I had no problem with him putting up some art if he wanted to. "Whatever you'd like. What kind of paintings do you have?" I imagined that he might like Van Gogh. I could probably find a decently sized print of his sunflowers to go over the couch in the living room if Eli would have wanted that.

But Eli gave me a look as if he didn't understand what I was asking him. Until his expression cleared. "Oh. No. I have pictures of the horses I've helped rescue or the ones I helped get adopted. I like to have them up. When I have a tough day, it's nice to be able to look at them and be reminded of the happy outcomes that are possible with all the hard work we do at the rescue. And you probably think that's stupid."

He was blushing heavily as he turned away from me, and I came up behind him to wrap my free hand around his stomach. He froze under my gentle touch, but I ignored that fact as I kissed the back of his neck and hoped that in time he would become far more relaxed around me.

"I don't think that's stupid at all. I wish I had something I could point to at the end of the day besides my bank account to tell me that the hours I spent with my clients and in airports and on airplanes was somehow worth it all."

I was envious of him having that, and of the selfless work that he did. I kissed the back of his neck again before I released him, but this time he moved to the side, giving me more access to his neck. I gently flicked my tongue out over his earlobe, and he giggled before pulling away. But instead of trying to get away from me, now he was just playing, and I wished I could enjoy the moment with him, but I was fairly certain that the ravioli would be done by now.

"Have you already eaten dinner?" I asked him.

"Do you have enough for two? I can go to the grocery store if you don't. That's not a big deal to me. I sort of eat cereal for most of my meals when I'm alone." He blushed from embarrassment this time, and I took his hand and led him back down the stairs.

I hadn't known when to expect him, but I had chosen something that was easy to divide just in case he'd arrived around dinnertime, and now I was glad that I had. "Take a seat at the island." I lacked a real dining table. I rarely saw the use for one, and instead of considering the benefits of one now, I poured him a glass of wine and got to plating dinner.

"For not even knowing how old I am, you sure like to give me alcohol."

I looked up from where I was plating the butternut squash ravioli to find him smiling at me. "I do, though. It's on your profile. Or, rather, your age range is. Twenty-three to twenty-seven."

He sipped his wine and didn't look nearly as put off by it as he had been with the red I'd given him before. Maybe he greatly preferred sweet white wines. "I'm twenty-five."

Nearly half my age. I knew better than to mention that, though. "How old were you when you first started using the app?"

"Perfectly legal to have sex, but not old enough for the beers I drank that night. But they helped. I wasn't nearly as nervous."

I'd stopped plating so that I could look at him across the island. "Were you capable of saying no, if you'd wanted to?"

Eli put his wine down. "Are you asking me if I was raped when I lost my virginity? Because if you are, then no, I wasn't. He was…. Fine. Most of the guys on the app aren't exactly nice, and I've found out since then that he's pretty much the norm when it comes to the guys there. But he wasn't mean about it either. He didn't know it was my first time, and I sure as hell didn't say anything about it. I was too nervous to even tell him my name at the time. I've since learned his, and he knows mine, but that's about it."

While I was glad that he hadn't been raped for his first time, I couldn't exactly understand how anyone would choose to use a hookup app as a way of losing their virginity. The whole concept was completely foreign to me. Hadn't he dated anyone who would have been a better bet for the first person he jumped into bed with than a complete stranger? I decided to hold off on my questions for a while. He was already doing more talking than I was used to.

"I hope you like ravioli," I said as I put his plate in front of him, with an apple and pecan salad in a small bowl beside his main plate. I came over with my dishes and our silverware to sit beside him on one of the stools.

He dug in, and I smiled at his obvious delight in a meal that was so simple. The ravioli had come from the grocery store down the hill. The sauce was just butter and a bit of brown sugar, and the salad had been prepackaged. It was an easy meal that had taken me fifteen minutes to make, most of which was waiting for the water to boil. I always forgot how long it took for water to heat up in Colorado. It had something to do with the altitude, just as baking never turned out quite right here unless I used the high-altitude directions. Thankfully I didn't run into that problem very often as I wasn't a baker. I rarely ever even cooked for myself, unless a simple meal like this counted.

"There's no reason for you to have to buy groceries with your own money while you're here, so I'll leave you a monthly cash allowance for food. If you want to cook for me while I'm here, too, I certainly won't turn you down."

He nodded and kept eating. "Is stuff like this what you usually eat, then?"

I didn't exactly have a preferred meal type. "I suppose so. A salad or vegetables with every meal and something else as well. What do you like to eat?"

I saw him smile out of the corner of my eye. He was nearly done with his dinner. "Really cheap pizza and cereal. Drive-through if I can afford it." He acted as if that kind of a lifestyle didn't bother him. I chose not to mention how unhealthy that type of a diet was for him. I imagined he'd probably heard it all before.

He finished dinner and seemed to hesitate for a moment before piling up his empty dishes and taking them to the sink. For a moment I thought he was just going to leave them in there and we'd have to have a talk about cleanliness, which I definitely was not looking forward to, but then he rinsed off his plate and bowl and put them in the dishwasher.

"The wineglasses should only be hand washed," I told him.

"Do you have wine with every meal?"

Did I? I hadn't really thought about that. And since I didn't like eating breakfast, I chose not to correct him there. "I often do with dinner, but not so much with lunch. Do you?" I knew the answer even as I was asking him.

He left the washed wineglass on the counter before turning around to face me. "I like soda, but I'm trying to drink more water. Evaline likes to lecture me about how unhealthy soda is when she sees me drinking one early in the morning. She doesn't know how late I'm up from the night before, and sometimes I need that boost of caffeine to even become functional. Orange juice is nice too, when I'm not dragging ass." He shoved his hands into the pockets of his jeans and leaned against the counter. "How do you really feel about me having friends over? Would you prefer that I do that only when I'm at my own place? He doesn't bother me when I have people over, if you were wondering about that, so I could go back to my place. No problem."

I'd finished eating, but I wasn't entirely sure what to say to him at that point. "Are you asking if you can bring guys from the app here to have sex with them? And while I'm here as well? Or are you asking if you can have a friend over to watch TV?"

He came over and leaned his forearms on the island. "If I'm going to be with someone, even when you're not here, I won't bring them here. I like having my space, and letting some random person know where to find me isn't part of that. But I have a best friend who also works at the rescue, and sometimes, though not often, we'll get together to watch a movie. That's what I'm asking about."

That made me feel better. I would be worried enough about him when I wasn't around. I wouldn't want to be questioning whether or not someone had treated him badly in my own house when I wasn't there.

"That's fine. But not while I'm home. Is that acceptable for you?"

"Of course." He shrugged. "This is your house. No reason you should have to put up with my friend when you're here trying to relax."

I smiled at him and was glad that he understood. I wanted my space as well. Living with a roommate was going to be an adjustment for us both. "What is your friend's name?"

"Mason."

I chuckled and got up to clean up my dishes. "Grayson and Mason. That doesn't leave you confused at all?"

Eli grinned. "Not at all. You see, Mason is twenty-one, short, skinny, and really naive. Like he's young, but he acts really young too. Sometimes I worry about just how new to the world he seems. And he hasn't come out to his parents yet. He's saving up money so that he can do it when he's already moved out. In case they throw a shit fit about him being gay."

"That's quite reasonable. Was waiting until he was in a better place and more independent his idea or yours?"

"Mine."

Eli's admission brought up a whole host of new questions that I wanted to ask him, but I also didn't want to pry or give him reason to leave my house, where I knew he was safe. He hadn't even removed his shoes. I didn't care if he brought dirt into the house, especially since I expected him to sweep the floors occasionally as part of keeping the house clean. But since he had his shoes on still, I had the impression that he was looking to run out of my front door even as he walked past me and went to go sit on my couch in the living room.

"What do you like to watch?" he called back.

"Anything you want. I need to leave early for my flight in the morning, so I won't be up too much later as it is, so if you find something, feel free to watch it. Would you like another glass of wine?" I poured myself another. I knew he'd washed his glass out already, but he could use another one if he wanted to.

Eli found a monster movie to watch. I was surprised that it was in black and white. Certainly there was a more recent *Frankenstein* adaptation that he would have enjoyed more.

"I like classic horror movies," he said as he kicked off his shoes, leaving himself in just his socked feet, which he pulled up under him.

I would not have expected that from him, and I realized I didn't know much about him at all actually. "What kind of music do you like, then?"

He briefly glanced at me before looking back at the screen. "Eighties rock ballads with the hair."

That was another surprise. I'd expected something far more recent. "Who turned you on to that kind of music? It's…." I wanted a word that wouldn't offend him but would still show my surprise at his choice. "Unusual for someone your age to prefer music that was around before you were born."

This time he seemed to be doing his best not to look at me as he leaned forward and rounded his shoulders a bit. "My dad."

Well, that was nice. I did want to know more about him, and this was a good direction to be going on. "Are you still close?"

He sighed heavily. "We never really were. He used to share all of his old records with me before he died. After, I just kept listening to them. But he died when I was seven, so I never really got to know him."

I reached over to him and was surprised when he jerked away from my brief touch against his shoulder, though I might have caused him some pain. "I'm sorry to hear that. Do you want to talk about him or how he died?"

Eli shook his head, but he did tell me anyway. The words were harsh, like they were being pulled out of him against his will. Like he didn't want to tell me anything more about his family or his past but he felt like he didn't have a choice in it either.

"He killed himself by overdosing. My mom remarried. I don't get along with her or her husband at all." He turned his head toward me, and I was taken aback at the sheer pain in his perfectly clear gaze. "Do you need me to keep answering your questions to stay with you tonight, or can I stop now?"

"Oh, Eli." I pulled him into my arms and against my chest. I'd never held him like that before, and now I wondered why I hadn't. Had we really never been like this before? Had I been keeping him at a distance just as he'd been doing to me? "You don't have to do anything but clean up after yourself to stay here with me. I don't expect anything more than that from you." He lay against my chest and quietly sat there half next to me and half on my lap for the rest of the movie.

It ended far too soon for my liking, and by the end of it, I'd only had him in my arms for perhaps half an hour. If that. But as soon as it was done, he got up from the couch. "I'd like to go upstairs now. And unpack. And get ready for bed."

It took me far longer than it should have to realize that he was asking me for my permission to be excused. "Eli, please treat this house as yours too. You're my roommate. Nothing more or less. I don't need to give you permission to go, and if you don't want to hang out with me some nights, that's perfectly acceptable too. We can get you a TV for your room so you can watch your own shows or movies if you want time alone. Okay?"

He nodded and, without saying anything else to me, headed upstairs. I sighed and leaned back against the couch. I hadn't expected everything to be fine on the first night. We were getting to know each other still, after all. But had I expected to hurt him? Not at all. Of course not. And I deeply regretted that.

I stayed downstairs and watched the follow-up movie to the *Frankenstein* one while I listened to him getting his things put away. He'd left the door partially open, but I couldn't see him from the angle I was at. So I watched the *Dracula* remake, which was far more recent than the Frankenstein one had been, but my attention was divided between the movie and listening to Eli.

It was a strange feeling, but I liked having him in my house. It seemed as if he belonged in my space, even after only a few hours of him being there, and I felt comfortable with him living there while I would be out of the state on business. I hoped that over the next three days when I wouldn't be at home, he'd start to feel more comfortable in my house as well. Because right now he clearly wasn't.

It was late when I headed upstairs. I'd half watched the entire *Dracula* movie, and counted it as one of the worst recreations of the old classic that I'd ever been subjected to. I had wanted to go upstairs to see if Eli needed any help, but I had also wanted to stay out of his way and give him some space if he needed it. I didn't want to intrude on his personal space and give him the impression that I wouldn't be leaving him alone at all while he was living with me. He was my roommate now, and I wanted to treat him like that and not as my lover as he had been for the past few months. The dynamics of our relationship had changed, but that didn't mean that my respect for him had, and above all I still wanted him to be happy.

I went upstairs and hesitated on the landing between our bedrooms with the bathroom in front of me. He had some soft music playing. It might have been one of the long love ballads from the eighties, but I didn't know enough about that kind of music to be able to tell the difference. It sounded soft and beautiful, though. I wanted to say something to him. I should have. But I wasn't sure what.

And while I was trying to come up with something to say to him, he came out of his bedroom with only a pair of loose shorts hanging around his hips, his toothbrush and toothpaste in his hand. He looked surprised to see me as he stood there in his bedroom doorway, and we stared at each other for a few seconds.

"Um. Hi," he began.

I recovered. A bit. "I wanted to say good night. I'll try not to wake you when I leave early tomorrow morning."

Eli leaned against the doorframe. "If you do, I'll probably be able to go right back to sleep." He hesitated, then stepped forward a bit until he was next to me. I held perfectly still as he kissed my cheek. "Thanks for letting me spend the night."

I watched him head into the bathroom, probably to finish getting ready for bed. "You're welcome here anytime. I like knowing that you're here and that no one is hurting you."

He smiled at me over his shoulder. "I do too." Then he closed the bathroom door, and I went into my room. I used the bathroom after him, and an hour later I was in my bed, alone, while I thought about Eli sleeping just down the hall from me.

CHAPTER NINE

Eli

GRAYSON WAS gone by the time I woke up the next morning. If he had managed to disturb my sleep while getting ready sometime before I got up close to nine, I hadn't noticed. Either that or I didn't wake up that much, because I didn't remember him leaving at all. He must have made some noise, though, and it did bother me that I hadn't been disturbed. Normally I really didn't sleep that well in new places. But Grayson's spare bed was soft, and once my mind had settled down, I hadn't had any trouble getting to sleep. I found the spare key he'd left for me on the island, and I had a glass of milk while I twirled it between my fingers.

We were roommates, I reminded myself. Not boyfriends. We weren't dating. But I was living with him. And, most importantly, I still had my independence. I tried to tell myself this arrangement didn't come with strings. I didn't believe that for a second, despite what Grayson had said to me the day before. But I knew that, if it did come down to it and he demanded sex from me like Brent had, Grayson had been given plenty of opportunities to hurt me, and he never had. He'd never shown even a hint of the aggression that Brent had so quickly jumped on. I'd still feel like a whore if Grayson asked me for that, but at least I wouldn't be a bloody, broken whore whose face was smashed up and whose whole body hurt, like I was right now because of Brent.

But since I was living with Grayson now, it would mean that, if it came to me trading my body for a place to live again that Grayson would have access to me whenever he was in town. He'd said that it wouldn't be all that often, but right now Brent only used me a few times a week. I didn't know if I could handle having Grayson around all day for multiple days in a row and demanding that I be with him anytime during that period. It took me so long to recover from being with Brent to the point where I was no longer shaking, and I needed that time to myself for my own sanity. If Grayson demanded that, I wouldn't get time away. And what about work? I still had to work. And my schedule couldn't be put around his.

And.... And.... And.... My mind was circling with possibilities, and I was starting to forget how to breathe properly.

I was getting ahead of myself, and I needed to get my racing thoughts under control. Grayson had said that being in his house meant that I didn't have to give him sex, and I would go with that until things changed. And when they did, because I fully expected Grayson to go back on his word to me like every other guy always did, then I'd deal with it then, and hopefully I'd have enough money saved up by then to be able to tell both he and Brent to fuck off and die.

First, though, I needed breakfast, which Grayson was sorely lacking in. He had some milk, which was almost expired and I'd already had some of. But after that there was nothing. He didn't even have any cookies for me to pretend were breakfast. I knew from the other times I'd been in Thornwood that there was a diner in town. It was really the only place to eat, and I'd driven past it the night before. They had to have something breakfast-like at Rosie's. I could get an omelet if nothing else.

I got showered and walked down the hill from Grayson's house to the diner. I could see it from the front porch, all shiny metal and a neon flashing sign, like we were in the fifties. That didn't bother me. Instead it made me hope that they had milkshakes. The good old-fashioned kind that were full of ice cream and real syrup instead of fake cheap stuff. I stuffed my hands into my pockets and turned onto the road to get to the diner. I had to pass the grocery store on the way there, and I decided to stop by before I went back to Grayson's house. But that would be after I got some breakfast into me.

Thornwood was tiny, like the kind of place that really had no business even calling itself a town because it was so small. I doubted it existed on any map. And I couldn't believe I was living there, even temporarily, because Trent lived there. It wasn't as if I hated him, and I'd even been to his boyfriend's place a few times to do follow-up yearly visits to make sure the horses Caleb adopted from the sanctuary were still doing okay. That was protocol. But it was hard not to be annoyed just being there because I knew how close he was at any given moment. I didn't hate him and I didn't love him. And when I wasn't in Thornwood, I really didn't think about it.

But seeing him there at the counter when I came in, surrounded by other cops, all of them in uniform, annoyed me for some reason. And my scowl didn't go away when I sat down either, because the only open place to sit was two stools down from him.

"Here's a menu, and what can I get you to drink, sugar?" a woman behind the bar, whose name tag said Roxie, asked me. She had to be in her sixties, and something about how kind her smile was made me not be so annoyed at the fact that Trent was so close to me. It was as if it was hard for me to be upset while she was around.

"Um." What did I want? I wasn't up for orange juice that morning, though that was my normal breakfast drink of choice. "Coffee? With milk but no sweetener?"

She gave me another smile. "You got it. I'll be right back to take your breakfast order."

"Thanks." I opened the menu and instantly found what I was looking for. There was my favorite breakfast food right on top of the menu. French toast with strawberries and powdered sugar, and the picture made it look amazing. I was practically drooling over the menu.

"Eli?"

I froze at the sound of Trent's voice, then slowly turned to look up at him. He'd moved from a few stools over to stand directly to my left. I swallowed quickly. "Hi."

He gave me a slight smile. Like he was uncomfortable being so close to me too. We weren't unfriendly, but I'd never go out of my way to try to be close to him again. I'd learned a lot since that one night years ago.

"Are you here to do a checkup on the horses?"

I would be doing exactly that, but not for a few more weeks at the soonest. "Not yet."

He shifted his weight and messed with his belt a little. I figured they were probably nervous gestures. As it was, I could barely remember to breathe again as long as he was standing so close to me. He made me nervous and uncomfortable, even at a distance.

"So what are you doing here?"

I laughed. Maybe that was a new nervous gesture for me. Or maybe he just made me crazy enough that I'd finally lost it. "Hoping to get some french toast for breakfast."

But Trent wasn't about to drop it. "This is a long way to go from Parker to get some breakfast, and I know for a fact that you have breakfast places in Parker. So let's try this again. What are you doing here?"

I stared at him for a long few moments. And then I glared at him. "I'm not going to do anything to your boyfriend."

"Husband," Trent corrected me instantly.

And suddenly, as if something got flicked inside of me, I felt so much better around him. He was married. I was unbelievably happy for him. "Congrats." I smiled up at him. I didn't really like Trent all that much, but I did like Caleb. He had a soft spot for kids and horses. Trent liked horses too, but I got a different vibe from Caleb.

"Thanks." He relaxed his looming stance a little too. Maybe he could sense the change in me as well. "So if you're not here to do another run-through of the barn and pastures, then why are you in Thornwood?"

I could have lied to him or continued to evade his questions. But I was hungry, Roxie was back and ready for my breakfast order, and the other cops were looking impatient as they got up around us and headed toward the front door.

"I'm staying with a friend here for a few days."

"Who?" he continued to press me. "And did you fall off a horse, or what the hell happened to your face?"

I was hungry, and now I'd had enough of his questions to last me for a long, long time. "Sure, I fell. Are you going to arrest me for being in your town and refusing to tell you who my friend is?"

Trent laughed, and it was real, unlike any of the other times that I had heard him laugh. "Take care, Eli. Be nice to my husband next time you're at the barn. No going into horse-rescue nazi mode anymore. You know him better than that now. It's been years."

I nodded, silently agreeing to hold back my usual hundred points that I'd often find wrong with the barns I had to evaluate. I was strict. I knew that. But it was for the good of the horses. But I supposed that Caleb had proven that he had good intentions over the years that he'd been fostering for the rescue. I could pull back a bit. Trent lifted his hand and brought it close to my shoulder like he was going to pat me, but I shied away, and he pulled back at the same time. Not being uncomfortable with him didn't extend to me also being okay with being touched by him. He seemed to get it, because he frowned and put even more space between us.

"I'm not interested in hurting you," he told me, his voice going quiet, maybe in an attempt to keep everyone in the diner from hearing us and gossiping about our business later. I had no doubt that this would be just the kind of town to do that. Cop Has Awkward Conversation with Mystery Man at Diner. I could see the headline now. Maybe we'd even make the front page. It wasn't something I was interested in seeing in the least.

I hoped Roxie wouldn't give up on me. I really did want that french toast. "I'm not afraid of you, but I don't like being near you either. It's complicated."

"You're still not over that I didn't send you any messages? But that was years ago. And I apologized for ignoring you. I thought we were all done with that."

Seriously? He wanted to recall our one-night stand now? In this diner? When I hadn't even had breakfast yet or so much as a sip of my quickly cooling coffee? Fuck that. "I'm not still upset about that," I hissed at him as quietly as I could. "Now go away."

"Fuck, you're an asshole," Trent grumbled at me. But at least he was walking away when he did so.

I rolled my eyes and plastered my best smile on my face for Roxie. "French toast please."

To her credit, she looked completely unconcerned with what Trent and I had been talking about as she wrote down my order in a little notebook she then put right back in her apron pocket.

"It's not my business—"

I held back my groan and tried not to let my smile slip while I waited for her to say whatever she thought she had any right to.

"—but Trent needs a good kick in the pants once in a while. His momma was my best friend, and I miss her dearly, but Caleb can only do so much to help him now. So if you've got something to say to him, I suggest you do it. He's not a bad boy, but he's got his moments where I wonder why he bothered getting out of bed at all if he's going to be in such a sour mood. You have my full permission to give him what for whenever you feel like it. Now, my Thomas on the other hand, he's a sweet boy. You see him walking around with a little girl and you best be nice to them. His boyfriend plays football. He's good too so you watch out if you think of being anything but nice to them. That is, if you're planning on sticking around here for more than just a bit of breakfast."

I stared at her as I nodded. So this was where all the gossip in town probably originated. Right here from a woman who looked like she was in her sixties and could still easily clobber me with a rolling pin if I crossed her.

"Thanks for the warning, but I don't plan to be in town long enough to really get to know anyone."

She shrugged and tapped the counter in front of me with her neatly manicured fingers. Which were painted pale pink and had little white hearts on them that were so crooked I thought a child must have painted them. Maybe the little girl she warned me about being nice to.

"Okay, sugar. You take it easy, and I'll be right back with your breakfast."

"Thank you." As she walked away, I took out my phone and began looking through my messages, most of them unfortunately from Hot Guy Hook Ups. Mason wanted to know if they'd caught the guy who had beaten me up yet. *They probably won't. I didn't give them much to go on,* I told him. It wasn't a complete lie. I really needed to get more friends because forty-two of my emails were from guys wanting to have sex with me, and my one text was from Mason. Well, hmmm, not all were from guys wanting me immediately at least. There was one from Grayson. *Good morning. I hope I didn't wake you when I left this morning.*

I'll schedule my planes later in the day from now on, he'd said. And he'd sent it around four that morning. That sounded like a miserable time to be awake unless I was going for a sunrise ride, like we sometimes did at the rescue.

Were we at the stage where we said good morning to each other? I was living with him, on an extremely temporary basis, so maybe we were. And yet that felt weird. Like it was too much and too fast and way too soon for me to be doing all this mushy crap with him. I didn't do this with anyone. Not even with Mason, and I'd known him for years. But I also didn't live with Mason.

But then again I also didn't have sex with Mason, and I hadn't spent a good chunk of last night curled up against his chest like I was a damn child in need of some serious comforting. Which I pretty much had been. It had been nuts and I'd felt crazy as I'd gone upstairs just to get some much-needed space to be able to think for a little while.

I could do this, I decided as I stared down at my phone. I could text him and not just message him through the app like we had always done before. I wasn't going to say good morning to him, but I could at least give him something more intimate than making our only way of connecting to each other sending messages with a damn hookup app. So I said hi and sent him back my phone number. Then my french toast arrived, and I dug into every sweet bite of it. After I covered it with maple syrup of course. The diner even had the good kind. The real stuff that wasn't watered down. I was practically ready to lick the plate by the time I was done eating my breakfast.

I left Roxie a big tip as I paid for my food, then headed out of the diner. My next stop was the grocery store. I had two more days at Grayson's before I decided if I wanted to stay with him for the rest of the month. I wasn't going to think any further ahead than that, except to remind myself how much I really needed to start saving up. Brent had given me a break on the rent, and Grayson was giving me another, but I had to take care of my own stuff from now on. I hated relying on other people, and this was already too much for me.

At the store I got a box of cookies and some stuff to make sandwiches. I knew how much was in my bank account, and I could have afforded real food. Plus Grayson had left me a few hundred in cash on the island. But I hadn't even touched that. Maybe if I stayed there more than the three days that he'd be gone, I would buy some food for him with his money. But I saw no reason to use it for just myself. And more than that, I didn't want to use it either. He didn't need to be buying me food. I could do that on my own. I just had to eat cheaply until I got my own place again.

By the time I got back to Grayson's house, I still had three more hours to kill before I needed to leave to get to work. It would take me about an hour and a half to get to Parker from Thornwood, but I was sure that Evaline wouldn't mind if I came in earlier. I could work as much as I wanted to, I just couldn't get paid for the extra hours. I didn't mind. The horses were the only ones that I was ever really comfortable around. I made myself a turkey sandwich, then left it wrapped up in the fridge so that I'd have it there when I got back to Grayson's house for a quick dinner. I was scheduled to be there until eight, so I knew I probably wouldn't get back until after nine. And I was scheduled for an early evaluation in Longmont the next morning. It was going to suck, but I really didn't mind it. Whatever would help the horses, I would always do for them.

I DIDN'T get back to Grayson's house until close to midnight because of an accident on I-25. I probably could have figured some way to go around the highway, but I really didn't know of any other way to get to Thornwood. So when I stumbled into his house, I was exhausted and cranky after a long day at work and a horribly long drive. I had enough time for a hot shower before I didn't bother to close the bedroom door behind myself.

THE NEXT morning I was still tired, since I'd had to get up at five to be on time for the adopter evaluation, but this time Mason was shadowing me, so it wasn't so bad. He'd had the previous day off work, and he hugged me as we got out of our cars and headed up the street to the potential adopter's house. Hugging each other wasn't exactly professional, but at seven in the morning, I was a bit too tired to care.

The adopter lived in Piney Creek Ranches, which was a subdivision I would have loved to own a house in because it was maybe twenty minutes from Denver, but everyone had a big house and a few acres of horse property. I could never afford to live in a place like this, though.

"Rich horse people," Mason quietly said as we walked up the side of the road and past a shiny white vinyl horse fence. A bay quarter horse was watching us as we passed by him. If he'd been closer, I would have reached over the fence to pet him. It wasn't good to pet strange horses, since they could and often would bite, but being bitten didn't bother me anymore. I'd been thrown, I'd broken bones, I'd been kicked, I'd been bitten, and I'd been stomped on lots of times. Horses could be dangerous and unpredictable. I was used to that. But I still loved them so freaking much anyway.

Mason hummed as he walked beside me, and I rolled my eyes even as I was smiling. "Cut it out when we get up there," I told him.

"Uh-huh. Your face doesn't look quite so awful today."

That was almost a compliment. "Thanks." We came up to the house, which looked like something I would have expected to see in Santa Fe, not in Colorado. A red tile roof complemented the white stucco and numerous arches. I thought it was pretty, but I much preferred the green pasture and the red barn beside it. I had my clipboard out, and I was already taking notes.

"What do you see?" I asked Mason, checking if he was picking up on the same areas that needed to be improved on the property. It wasn't a lot, but there were a few things that needed to be looked at before they could be approved to adopt from Green Acres. Which meant that if they wanted to still adopt that horse, I'd need to come back out. I hated making return trips, especially since I had a whole list of common problems to look out for on the website. I wanted the horses to get adopted, but if people couldn't follow even the simple directions that I put up to help them and the horses out, I started to get annoyed. I didn't like wasting my time, and I already knew that I'd have to come back to do a recheck if they still wanted to adopt from us.

"Holes in the pasture need filling in," Mason started.

I'd noticed the three of them already. "Why?"

"Dangerous to the horses. They could trip and fall and break a bone or go lame from stepping in one of them."

I smiled. Mason was young, but he wasn't dumb, and he cared about the horses too. He also didn't try to talk over me or treat me like a moron because I was just twenty-five, and most of the people at the sanctuary were much older than me so they thought they ruled the world, or at least the little part of it that gave them full control at the rescue. The problem for those people was that I had the most seniority at the rescue because Evaline trusted me most and liked me and my work. That's why, when she wasn't there, I was in charge. And she was gone a lot, working with other rescues and bringing back horses from slaughter auctions around the country.

"The barn's roof is also missing a few shingles," Mason continued on.

I actually hadn't noticed that. "Good job. Now let's go meet them."

Meeting the Johnsons went well. They wanted a horse for their teenage daughter, which I never really liked, since the horses often ended up back with us after the kid went to college, but they also had an eight-year-old son who wanted to ride too, so he'd get the horse after the daughter went to college. I was horrible with names and didn't even really try learning them. Horses I was good with. People were a different story. Mason, though, didn't have that problem. He was a natural with them, and I liked having him there as my backup. Especially when I was as tired as I was that morning, because by the time the assessment was done, and we'd spent three hours in their house and walking around their property and talking about what kinds of horses would be best for their family and the light trail riding they wanted to do with the horse, I was ready to go back to bed.

As I was lying in bed, trying to fall asleep despite the bright sunlight coming in through the window beside me, Grayson called me. At first, since I was barely awake, I thought it was Mason, but then I realized he hated to call. He was a texter, just like me. So I answered it, expecting something horrible like him telling me I had to get out of his house because he didn't even like the thought of me there. Only, if he had said that, I was pretty sure that I was too tired to have cared at that point. These late nights and early mornings were a killer.

"Hello?" I answered his call.

"You sound like you're unwell. Are you okay?"

I couldn't hold back my yawn. "Yeah, I'm good. Just laying down for a bit. It was a late night, and then I had a really early morning. Well, not early for you, judging by how early you got up to go to the airport, but early for me."

He chuckled, but the sound seemed like he might have been nervous about something.

"What's going on with you?" I turned over on the bed and instantly regretted it as that gave my cock some friction. Talking to him got me kind of hard, but thinking about him while I was naked and lying in bed in his house definitely didn't help matters at all. Maybe I'd take care of myself when we were off the phone.

"Were you with the person who likes to leave bruises on you?"

So that's why he sounded strange. He was worried about me and my stupid choices while he wasn't there to babysit me. Huh. "No. I haven't seen him in a little bit."

"That's good." He sounded relieved now. "So you were working late?"

I nodded against the pillow. "Yes. Late night and then an early-morning home assessment today." And I was so tired. Did we really need to talk about this right now? All I wanted was to take a nap as soon as possible.

"I wish I could be at home with you. It was nice spending the evening with you."

I smiled. "It was. Wasn't it?" Aside from the part where he'd pushed too far, too fast and I'd broken down and needed to be by myself for a while, it had been almost fun.

"What are your plans for the rest of the day?"

"A seriously long nap. I don't have to be at work anymore today, so I'm actually off until the day after tomorrow. I'll probably watch some movies, walk around naked for a while...."

I heard Grayson's sharp intake of breath, and I laughed, because I was hoping to get that reaction from him. "I wish I could be there to see that."

I was sure that he did. Too bad I'd only been half serious about it. "Are you on a break?"

"Having lunch between meetings. Sushi. Do you like it?"

Raw fish? Not really. Not when I lived in Colorado and all the fish I ate was previously frozen. That's why I liked pizza and good beer when I could afford it. We were known for our Colorado pizza and our craft beers and homebrewers.

"Not really," I admitted. I shouldn't have felt bad about not liking raw fish. But I suddenly felt kind of out of place, like it was one more thing that separated us. Not like we had a lot in common to begin with. He was a lot older than me, he'd been through college, he had at least some money, which I absolutely didn't, and he apparently liked his raw fish. I shuddered.

"I'm having mochi ice cream for dessert. Do you like ice cream?"

To me it sounded like he was grasping at straws now to come up with something we both liked. Fortunately for him, I did like ice cream. I didn't have the slightest idea what mochi was, but I figured that ice cream was ice cream. And I could probably get behind that.

"I like mint chocolate chip. Or mint with cookies in it." And now I really wished that I'd grabbed some ice cream while I was at the store. I groaned, and it sounded far more like a sex sound than I'd meant it to.

He gasped, and I blushed. I hadn't meant to take the conversation there, but he seemed to have no problem going there. "Tell me what you're wearing."

That was a dangerous question, for both of us. "Nothing," I quietly admitted.

He hissed in his breath, and I wanted him to make that sound again, because it was just like the one he made when he was pushing inside of me for the first time during the night. I lifted up my hips and slid my hand between my legs to cup myself.

"Make that sound again. Please," Grayson practically moaned in my ear.

I hadn't realized that I'd made any sound at all. "Are you alone?"

"I am. I had the sushi delivered to my hotel room. I'm going to the bed now and opening my pants. What are you doing?"

"Stroking myself against the bed."

Grayson chuckled, and he sounded a bit breathless. "I wish I had you in my bed and under me right now. I'd push you down onto the mattress and slide into your ass."

Were we about to have phone sex? I'd never done that before. I didn't even know how to begin. "Um. I'd…." What would I do? "I'd moan." That sounded absolutely pathetic. Clearly I sucked at phone sex. "I'd…." Be really stupid about this.

"Come for me," he hissed, warming me up right away. And then it didn't matter what I said because I did know how to stroke myself, and my moans were always natural. If I ever did try to fake my moans, I was pretty sure I'd fail badly, and then someone would call me out on it. I thought about him thrusting inside of me like when he had me up against the wall. He was so much bigger than me, and when he had his arms up on either side of me by my head, I couldn't see anything but his arms. He became everything to me, and I liked not being able to focus on anything else. I needed that sometimes.

I whimpered as I thought about him deep inside of me, his mouth against mine as I panted against his lips, and his big hands running over my chest and stomach. I always got sweaty with him, and since I'd never showered with him before the last time, I'd been able to drive back home with our come mixing on my skin and my sweat dampening my clothes. With Grayson I'd never been in a hurry to wash him off my skin. Instead I'd almost savored him being there with me as I'd taken my time to clean myself.

I heard him getting closer. His groans became deeper, rougher, and I pictured him squeezing his thick cock between his fingers. "Are you thinking about me?" I asked him. I was so close too, just hearing him and his pleasure.

"Of course. You under me. You on your knees. My hands in your hair. Your gorgeous mouth over me as I feed my cock between your lips."

I closed my eyes and fought back my orgasm. But it was nearly impossible to do when he so obviously wanted me. I loved to be wanted. I was so often used and discarded that being wanted was a completely novel experience to me, and I didn't remember another guy that I'd been with who made it completely clear to me that he wanted just me like Grayson did.

I came with a cry that I half buried into the pillow. I rolled over onto my side as I shook. I didn't like lying in my own wet mess.

He panted my name and then came too, groaning into the phone. "Eli...."

I nodded. I didn't really know what to say either. "Thank you?"

He laughed, and I smiled as I tried to quiet my breathing. I wasn't doing a very good job of it, though. "Yes. Thank you. Are you going to go shower now? Or do you take a bath normally when you're alone?" Grayson asked.

When I had the energy, I'd shower. But now I desperately needed that nap that he'd interrupted. I was so glad that he had too. "I'll shower later. Nap now. Nice long nap."

Grayson chuckled. I could practically hear the smile in his voice. "I'll be showering now. Take care of yourself. I'll be home the day after tomorrow. We should go out to dinner when I get back."

I shrugged. I only cared about my quickly approaching nap, but I liked where his mind was. His simple words reminded me that I wasn't just good for sex with him. "Sure. Food. Could be good." I yawned loudly and made no attempt to cover my mouth to muffle the sound. "Bye now, though."

"Of course. Have a good nap, Eli. I'm glad I called you."

I smacked my lips together and pulled the pillow farther under my head. "Me too. Bye." I hung up and was asleep in a few minutes.

CHAPTER TEN

Grayson

I WAS home by two, thanks to taking an earlier flight to get away from a big storm that had been creeping up the East Coast. When I got there, I was disappointed to see that Eli wasn't, but I assumed he'd had to work. So I walked around my house instead to see if it felt different now that someone else was living in it.

Everything was neat, but some things were not where I'd left them. The TV remote was on the ottoman. I liked it on the TV stand. And when I turned it on, I noticed that Eli had left it on the crime drama channel. The smell of microwave popcorn lingered in the kitchen, but there was no other evidence of it, and I wondered if that had been his idea of lunch. I wanted him to eat healthier foods. I wasn't about to try to control what he did or ate, though, so that was just wishful thinking on my part.

I went upstairs and checked the bathroom. I saw one of the towels hanging up to dry, and there was a blue toothbrush lying on the sink. Mine was kept in a glass. His bedroom door was closed, and as much as I wanted to, I resisted the urge to go in there and invade his privacy, only to assuage my own curiosity.

They weren't large changes, but they were the signs that someone had lived in the house in my absence. And having those little additions to my house made me happy in a way I hadn't expected.

I showered to get the stink of the airplanes and airports off of me. Too many people around me always made me feel a bit dirty, and airplanes were the worst for that. Hundreds of people sharing their germs all at once and no way to get away from them. It was a germaphobe's worst nightmare. For me it was a necessary nuisance.

As I was drying myself off, I heard the front door open and close, followed by heavy footsteps, like Eli was wearing boots. I put on a sweater and a pair of jeans. I came out of my room and found Eli sitting down in the front entrance as he tried to pull a pair of cowboy boots off his feet. He was struggling and kept wincing as if he was sore.

I hurried downstairs and crouched in front of him, ready to help. "Hey," he said, leaning against the wall and letting me take over as I began pulling his right boot off, despite the dirt caked onto it.

"Hello. Will I be upset about why you seem hurt?" I hoped he hadn't made any ridiculous choices, including going back to his old apartment and whatever waited for him there.

Eli gave me a long look, then smiled. "Sorry. I'm tired. It took me a second to figure out what you were asking me. I thought for a moment there that you were going to be pissed about a horse throwing me. Don't worry, Grayson, I haven't been back to my place since I came to stay with you. I got bucked off and landed in the steel round pen fencing today. Hurt like hell, but I'll be okay. It just happened an hour and a half ago so that's why I'm still in so much freaking pain."

I was relieved to know it had only been a horse that had caused his pain, though that was bad enough. "Are you always getting thrown? It seems to me that you fall off more than should be normal for someone who likes to ride horses." I had his first boot off and moved to the second.

He laughed, then stopped abruptly and rubbed at his ribs. "That's not good. Ow. Yeah, I get thrown a lot. But I'm also the one who works with the young or inexperienced horses. We call them green horses. I get to evaluate them, and I know enough to do some training. Today's ride was going just fine too. Excalibur, that's the gelding I was riding, was doing just fine. He's got some problems that will need to be fixed, but he's not awful. But then a car backfired down the street, and he flipped out and bolted toward the wall. I tried to pull him away from the fence since I didn't want him to get hurt, but then he swung hard to the left and I fell sideways since I'd been balanced so far forward and really didn't have any stability. I think I need a bath, some painkillers, and a good night's sleep. Then I'll be all better."

It sounded incredibly dangerous, and I also tried not to be disappointed that I wouldn't get to have dinner out with him. "That seems like a good plan. May I help you up? Then we can go get something to eat."

"Sure." Eli smiled at me and offered me his hands. I helped him to his feet, and he picked up his boots to take them upstairs. I didn't even care that they were filthy and coming through my house as he headed upstairs. "I'll be ready in a half hour. Pick where you want to go. Please."

I should have been more concerned about him and less interested in still going out to dinner with him. But I couldn't help smiling. I'd been looking forward to going out with him since we'd decided to days before, and my desire to have him to myself had only increased in the hours leading up to the moment I'd gotten off the plane at Denver International Airport.

"Only if you think you'll be okay."

Eli laughed, then winced as he looked over the landing at me. "It's fine. This isn't even close to the first time a horse has thrown me into something hard. Nothing's broken. I'm just bruised. And at least this time you see me with bruises, it's because of a good thing. I was working with a horse, and now we know he spooks at car noises. That'll be good for the new owner to know. When he gets adopted."

"I admire your optimism," I told him as he headed into the bathroom.

"Being around the horses makes me happy. They don't expect anything out of me." Eli went into the bathroom seconds later, and I took out my phone to find somewhere that would be good for us to have dinner.

I settled on a steakhouse as he was coming out of the bathroom, this time with just a towel wrapped around his hips. He had a bright purple bruise on the left side of his ribs, but he didn't seem to notice it as he leaned over the railing and looked down at me where I was sitting on the couch with my socked feet up at the ottoman.

"What did you pick for us for dinner?"

I didn't say anything for a few moments since I couldn't keep myself from staring at him. He looked great in just the towel with nearly all of his muscles on display. He was lean and toned, and I missed getting to touch all of his smooth skin and feeling him jump under my hands.

"Grayson?"

I pulled my attention away from his stomach and the barely there trail of hair I knew would flow right under his towel, even though I couldn't see that hair now. "Yes?"

Eli was grinning at me. "Food?"

"Steak."

He nodded and went into his bedroom to get dressed. With him gone, it gave me a break to think clearly for the first time since he'd come through the front door. Part of me wanted to have him naked all night, and I would order in for us. I knew that we could have fun then. But he was bruised, again, and I had wanted to take him out to a restaurant for dinner instead of keeping him in my house. There would be time enough for that later. I wanted to treat Eli to a nice meal for tonight.

Eli came down a few minutes later, wearing a T-shirt and a pair of jeans that were fairly clean. I was starting to realize that most of his jeans had dirt from working with the horses embedded into the fibers. They'd likely never get as clean as they were to begin with. And, surprisingly, I was okay with that. I made sure that I was always well dressed and clean, but Eli had a reason for having dirt on his jeans and around his cuticles. It wasn't that he was sloppy or simply didn't care. His reason was he worked hard and spent his days outside with horses that needed help.

He winced as he sat down on the couch next to me. We were only six inches apart, but I would have preferred us to be closer. We still had hours before I'd take him out to dinner. Even if I made it an early date, we still wouldn't be leaving the house for at least an hour.

So I took a chance and put my arm around his shoulders to see how much he would allow. If we were having sex, I knew I would have free rein with him and that I could do whatever I wanted to him as long as he still enjoyed it. But this wasn't sex. This was me wanting to touch him in a friendly environment that lacked any sexual intimacy. And I felt the moment he tensed as I laid my hand against his shoulder.

I pulled back instantly but he shook his head. "It's okay. I'm not used to being touched by someone who isn't Mason and when sex isn't involved. It's weird, but it's okay."

With him giving me that explanation, I returned my hand to his shoulder, and after a few minutes, I pulled him close against my side. He closed his eyes and laid his head back over my arm. That pinned my arm to the couch, and I knew it would become uncomfortable in a while, but for the moment I loved the simple, intimate act of sitting so close together on the couch as if we were a couple and not just friends who had sex.

"How were your flights?" he asked me. He still didn't have his eyes open.

I smiled at him, even though he couldn't see my expression unless he was peeking. "They were good. No turbulence at all really, which is surprising coming away from the mountains. How was having the house to yourself?"

He got a soft smile across his face. "Quiet. It was nice not to have neighbors, and to be alone for a little while." He popped open his eyes. "I'm sorry. Not that I meant that I wasn't glad that you were back. It's your house after all. And—"

Eli tried to sit up, but I placed my hand gently across his chest, holding him there against the back of the couch, and my arm, for a little while longer. "It's fine. I knew what you meant. I haven't lived in an apartment since I graduated from college, but I can imagine how it must be for you. I certainly didn't enjoy it when I had to live there."

"What college did you go to?" he asked. I was glad that he was becoming more curious about me. I had so many questions for him. I wanted to know about his life, more about his family, his hobbies outside of listening to eighties music, watching old horror movies, and working with horses.

"Yale." I was proud of my education and my degree. "I went in on a scholarship. Where did you go?"

He turned his head to look at me, and I traced the smooth muscles up his chest to the side of his neck. "I didn't. I barely graduated from high school." I stilled my hand against his skin, and he must have been able to tell how surprised I was by his admission, because he sighed. "Is my lack of a college degree going to be a problem for you?" Eli asked me bluntly.

I shook my head. I saw no reason why it would be. "I was surprised, but I don't think less of you for not going to school. Was it a matter of finances?" I had to stop myself right there. I was surprised at how easy it had been for me to leap in and begin to offer to pay for his college degree. Not that I couldn't afford to, especially now that I wasn't paying a mortgage of any kind, but it was more that I'd already realized how independent Eli was, and I didn't want to offend him with my offer. I also didn't want him to think that my offer would come with any strings.

"No. I just never saw much use for it." He turned so that he was facing me on the couch, with his legs pulled up under him. It put his cheek against my arm instead of the back of his head. I laid my hand on his thigh instead. He didn't ask me to move it. "I started working at Green Acres not long after I finished high school. Evaline needed a full-time assistant and offered to train me and give me a place to stay if I worked my ass off for her and the horses. I did everything I could for her until the rescue got to be too big for just the two of us. Then she helped me get an apartment nearby and on the bus route so that I could get there back when I didn't have a car. The rescue grew fast, especially once a big neglect case hit. Then she was overrun, but she loved it. The point I'm trying to make here is that all the schooling I've ever needed was what Evaline gave me, and the only job I've ever wanted is at the rescue. I'll be her assistant until she's no longer able to take care of it, and then when that happens, then it becomes mine to be carried out under her directions."

He shrugged to finish off his bout of information, and I simply stared at him. He had everything he ever wanted, and it was so different than what I did. I enjoyed my expensive meals and my luxury car and my fine suits. He was perfectly content working with horses all day.

"You really are happy working there. Aren't you?"

Eli smiled at me as if he absolutely was. It was the contented kind of smile of someone who had everything they'd ever wanted in life, and I was envious of him. "I am. If you ever want to come do some actual work with the horses, I could show you around a bit. You wouldn't be able to ride any of them, because of legal reasons and liability stuff, but you could pet them, and I could introduce you to my favorites."

I didn't have the shoes, the shirt, or the pants for such an adventure, but I nodded anyway. Getting to be a part of his world, in whatever fashion he'd let me, meant more to me than any pair of shoes that would likely be ruined by going to a barn with him.

"Are you going to make me clean out stalls?"

Eli laughed and shook his head. The action made his hair fall over his eyes, and I reached up and brushed his hair back before he could raise his hand to do just that. He blushed and ducked his head a bit, but that made his hair fall even more forward, so I gave up and simply ran my fingers through his hair as he brought his head against my shoulder.

"I only make the people who annoy me muck out the barn. So don't annoy me, and I won't make you shovel horse shit."

I chuckled and pulled him closer. Then I tilted his head back so that I could kiss him. I let my mouth linger over his as I tasted him and the toothpaste he'd just used before coming down. I used mint. He apparently liked cinnamon. I didn't like that taste, but I knew that I would put up with it as long as I got to keep kissing him.

Someone knocked on my front door, interrupting us, and I sighed as I got up to answer it. Eli had a full-blown pout across his bottom lip as he watched me go to the door. He might have meant his expression to be cute and perhaps a little sexy. But watching him pout, and knowing he was sad because I was no longer kissing him, went straight to my cock.

I shook my head as I opened the door, but I froze as I saw Nigel there on the other side, standing on my front porch with a bottle of red wine in his hand. "Welcome back to Colorado. I thought we could catch up. It's been a few weeks since I saw you last." He let himself into my house, and I looked between Nigel and Eli as I wondered how quickly I could get Nigel out of my house so that I could get back to giving Eli all of my attention.

CHAPTER ELEVEN

Eli

I LOOKED at the well-dressed man who was about the same age as Grayson and also black, and I realized they were probably friends and I had no reason to be jealous or uncomfortable with whatever-his-name-was being there. Grayson looked just as surprised at him showing up as I felt, but I was mostly annoyed that I didn't get to keep kissing Grayson because he was there.

"Nigel, this is Eli. Eli, this is my friend Nigel."

So he was just a friend, then. That was pretty obvious actually. I'd seen the profiles of the guys Grayson had been with on the app, and Nigel wasn't even in the right age range. He liked his guys a lot like me. Twenties to thirties, a little muscular, and white. That didn't bother me. But the way Nigel was looking at me, like I was a particularly interesting puzzle, was starting to unnerve me.

"So you're Grayson's bit of rough. Well, you're certainly pretty enough." Nigel put the bottle of wine down on the island and went over to grab a few glasses. "Do you care for wine, Eli?"

I got off the couch to go stand closer to Grayson. "No, but thank you." Things were tense enough without Grayson clamming up, so I wished that he would snap out of it sooner rather than later.

"Not old enough to drink yet?" Nigel taunted me. And I knew it was a taunt because of the sharklike grin he gave me at the end as if he was daring me to say, or do, something that would piss Grayson off enough to get me thrown out on my ass.

But I just smiled at him, giving him the same expression I reserved for people who wanted to adopt but I thought would be better off with a plastic model horse than a real horse that would likely kill them with their own stupidity.

"No, I'm old enough. I just don't like the taste of red. What's a 'bit of rough'?" I was sure that it was an insult of some kind. But I wanted to know exactly how I was being insulted before I got all upset about it.

"He's implying that I'm slumming it with you," Grayson quietly told me.

Oh. Was that really all it was? Well, okay, then. "You are. So that makes sense." I figured it was time to be extra nice to the person who had tried to insult me and failed. "Nigel, we were going to go out for steaks. Would you like to join us?" I wanted Grayson to see how much I could handle, how strong I really was, and how meeting his friend, even unexpectedly, didn't have to ruin my evening with him. I still wanted dinner. And I still wanted him in bed with me that night.

"I am—"

Whatever Grayson was going to say got cut off by Nigel. "No, thank you. I like to dine at places that might be a bit too highbrow for you. What do your parents do?"

That was a sensitive subject, and I didn't need the added insult. I looked to Grayson to assist me in this since his friend was being intentionally mean now.

"No answer? How about where you went to college? Or did you not graduate from high school?"

I gave Grayson exactly three seconds to say something in my defense. Anything. I would have taken him throwing Nigel out of the house, but aside from that, a good word about me would have been nice too. I had good qualities. He could have used any of them. By the third second, I would have taken him telling Nigel how good I was in bed, just so he said something.

But he didn't. He just stood there, looking like a statue. So I went upstairs to grab my sneakers and headed back down to the front door. Grayson still hadn't said anything.

"Actually, you two have fun. I forgot that I have to do a house assessment tonight. Sorry, Grayson, another time for dinner would be better. See you, Nigel." I grabbed my phone, my keys, and my wallet, and then I was gone. I stormed down Grayson's driveway and away from his house. I wasn't in the right frame of mind to drive so I walked. I cut into the woods to avoid people, especially if either of them decided to get in their cars to come looking for me. I was so tempted to slash Nigel's tires, but I refrained. To me, a person's friends were a reflection of themselves. Grayson wouldn't have kept Nigel around if he didn't get along with him, and for him to be able to stand Nigel, that meant he had to have something in common with him. So ten minutes into my storm-off session, I was convinced that there were two Graysons. There was the one I saw who was sweet to me. Then there was the one who thought I was beneath him and likely couldn't be trusted to eat at the same table without making a complete mess of the dinner and an utter fool of myself. And if that was the case, then I didn't want anything to do with either half of him.

For some reason I found myself near Caleb's house, not that being there was all that surprising. It was too small of a town to really get lost in. I was probably more likely to get eaten by a mountain lion than to actually lose my way. It hadn't even taken me twenty minutes to get to his brightly lit magazine-style log cabin.

With a sigh I knocked on the door. I didn't need to see his barn or his horses, but I did need an excuse to be somewhere and cool off, and being around horses always did that for me. Caleb's horses were the only ones I could get access to at such short notice, and besides, I didn't think he would really mind.

Thankfully Caleb, and not one of the other people I could hear talking inside, came to the door. "Eli? What are you doing here?" There was more worry than accusation in his voice. Maybe I looked like shit or something. I didn't think I'd been crying enough for someone to notice, but I could have very easily been wrong about that, just as I had been about Grayson actually liking me for more than just sex.

"Surprise horse well-being and barn inspection." Never mind that I didn't have a clipboard, and that I was dressed like I was going out.

Caleb looked me up and down and opened his mouth like he was going to protest, but I beat him to it.

"By fostering and adopting any horses from Green Acres, you give their representative, that's me, access to assess the horse or horses in your care and the property they're on, for any signs of mistreatment or, in the case of property, repair."

Caleb held his hands up in defense. "I know what I signed. You nazi. Come on down to the barn. I was just surprised to see you." He shut the door behind himself, and I followed him down the driveway to the slight hill and into the barn, where a big gray gelding, a paint gelding, a blue roan gelding, and a black mare stood in their stalls. The gray and paint geldings had been part of the rescue. I didn't know who the other two horses belonged to but I assumed Caleb's nephews, who had moved in with him at some point. I didn't follow his family drama at all, and I had no interest in it.

I let myself into the paint's stall. His name was Hawk, and Caleb had been taking care of him for years. He'd adopted him, just like he had with the gray gelding. The stall door rattled as I closed it behind myself, and Hawk tossed his head and put his ears back in irritation.

"Easy," I told him gently as I ran my hands in long, soothing strokes over his neck and shoulders. He looked great. I didn't need to be there. But since Caleb was still watching me, I had to go through the motions of making sure he was okay. So I ran my hands over each of his legs. "Any lameness?"

"None."

I could tell that just by touching the thin muscles over his legs. They were powerful, but they were stretched thin over long bones that were made for running, jumping, and getting hurt easily.

"How's his temperament? Any issues with training?"

"He's stubborn, but we're being patient with him. He's smart, too, which is a bad combination when we ask him to do something, like take a bit, and he knows how to knock us over to get away from doing anything we want him to." He chuckled, and I was glad he didn't seem angry about it at all. "Now, you want to tell me why you're really here?"

I bit back a sigh and continued my pretend evaluation of Hawk by walking around him. He was absolutely beautiful, with big white patches over his red coat. I loved paint horses and all the varieties they came in.

"I already told you. I'm assessing. You don't have to be here for this."

Caleb came over and leaned on the stall door so that we were looking at each other. "Actually, I think I do. Does this have something to do with Trent? Do you still care about him?"

I laughed so hard Hawk flattened his ears against his head and tried to run at the door where Caleb was standing. He didn't get up enough speed to really get far, so I was able to get between him and the door and push against his chest.

"Whoa. Easy there, big boy. I'm sorry. My mistake." I stroked his neck and his face while I kept apologizing to him until he was much calmer. "There you go. Good boy. That's a good boy." When he was all better, I looked back over at Caleb. "I don't want Trent. That has nothing to do with this."

"And you're not going to tell me what this is, are you?" he asked me.

I shook my head, but part of me wanted to talk to Caleb. He was a semineutral party, and he got along with horses. To me that meant I could maybe share some of what I was going through.

"I just…. You ever feel like you need to be with someone who doesn't expect anything from you? Well, that's how the horses are to me. I'm tired of…." I couldn't say having sex with people who didn't give a damn about me. As much as I liked Caleb, I didn't know him well enough to share something like that with him. "Being used," I decided to finish off by saying.

Caleb straightened up and gave me a nod, like maybe some part of him did understand. "I get it. Take all the time you need. When you're done, come up to the house and let me know you're leaving. Okay? Just don't fall asleep out here."

I laughed shakily, though I did keep my voice much quieter this time around. "Sure. I'll come say bye."

"Okay."

Caleb stepped back, and for the next hour, I had Hawk all to myself until Trent came into the barn.

"Caleb said I'd have as long as I needed," I protested even before Trent was able to say anything.

"Yeah, but that was before Grayson Pendleton reported you missing."

I groaned and leaned against the wall of the stall, which still kept a sleepy Hawk between us as he lightly dozed. "I was gone for less than two hours. And I'm an adult. Aren't there rules about calling people 'missing' in this situation?"

Trent smiled at me. "Sure, if this was Denver. But here if some guy says his boyfriend ran away, we tend to notice. Especially if that boyfriend is hiding out in my husband's barn. So how long have you been dating Grayson?"

I was surprised anyone would use that term to describe us. "We're not."

"Eli…." He was acting like he was trying to warn me away from lying to him since he was a cop.

Too bad for him I'd just about hit my limit with the whole human race for the night. "We're not dating. We met on the app. I'm his live-in fuck toy." Being blunt with him seemed to work because instead of saying anything else to me, he just blinked.

It took him a good five minutes to recover enough to speak to me again. "Do you want a ride back up to his house? Assuming that you're going back there tonight?"

I'd need to run by there to get my car at the very least. Then I could figure out how to get my stuff another time after I was back in my apartment. But going back to my place made me want to hurl at the thought of Brent being there, waiting for me to get home and coming over uninvited to hurt me again in whatever sick, twisted way he wanted. I'd had three whole days without him, and they'd been pretty perfect overall, up until tonight when Nigel had to come in and ruin it for us.

"Sure. I might as well go back. Thank Caleb for me please? For letting me hang out with Hawk for an hour?"

"Yeah. No problem. Do you want to talk about stuff?"

I shook my head as I came out of the stall and walked beside him up to his cruiser. He unlocked it, and I got in the front without asking him if that was okay. I'd never been arrested, so I'd never sat in the back of a cop car, and I wasn't about to start now. It smelled like old diner takeout food, and I thought he seriously needed to get it detailed.

"You used to be so happy. That night we met, you were practically bubbly. What happened to you, Eli?" Trent asked me even though I thought I'd made it pretty clear that I didn't want to talk to him about anything. But he was driving and asking me questions. I only had to hold out for a few minutes. But maybe talking to him would feel better. Maybe I'd get a reaction out of him when he actually knew the whole truth about our one night together.

"I learned that men are only interested in sex."

He shrugged like it was no big deal. "Guys from the app generally are. But—"

"I haven't been with anyone who wasn't on the app." I cut into whatever he was going to say.

Trent shot me a look. "But…. But…." He was starting to connect the dots. "You were an app virgin when we met. Bright shiny new unfilled heart on your profile. I remember it because it wasn't a symbol I'd seen before. I had to look it up to see what it meant."

"I was a *virgin* virgin when we were together," I clarified for him. And the guys had all been just like him. Very few of them wanted my name. None of them really cared what I liked or if they were being too rough for me. If they were hurting me. I used a plug so that they couldn't rush me, and I brought condoms with me so I stayed safe. Other than that, I didn't make the rules. Sometimes I'd go to meet with one guy, and he'd have friends there, and I'd stay because I didn't want them to laugh at me. Sometimes the guy would be way older than he said he was. And sometimes I got slapped around a bit while I was being fucked. It was just sex. Just guys using other guys like how it always was.

Trent stopped the car on the side of the road, then turned to me. "Eli. Shit. I'm sorry. I was an asshole back then. According to Caleb, I still am sometimes. I didn't know… I should have never treated you like that."

I shook my head. I knew better than that now. "Guys treat each other like things to be used. That's how the world works. You were just the first to show me that. I'm not mad at you for that. I just don't want to revisit it with you."

104

Trent reached for my hand, but I pulled it back quickly. I definitely did not want him touching me tonight, not when I felt so raw and flayed open. I'd thought Grayson was different, but he wasn't. Not really. He'd been nicer than the others, but I'd still been his thing to fuck when he wanted.

"Maybe instead of blaming all the other guys, why don't you ask yourself why you are only with people who use the app? I know people on there can be assholes. I was one of them. But you've got the choice not to be with them. You could just uninstall the app and go download a new one from one of those dating sites that says they get people married."

I groaned. Marriage absolutely wasn't for me. At least not right now. Maybe not ever. But he did have a point. "Are some people not like that, then?"

"Are you asking me if most guys won't just use you if they get the chance? Because no, there will always be people like that out there. The trick is to figure out how to stand up for yourself and decide that you don't want them to be like that with you."

I eyed him warily. He'd been one of those guys for me. He'd been the first of those guys. And every guy after him had been a repeat of how I'd felt with Trent when he refused to return my messages or see me again. Had I let myself be used all this time? And, if I had, did that mean that I'd somehow not only allowed it, and accepted the behavior of the other guys, but that I'd wanted it? Was my self-esteem really that fucked up?

"It's just something to think about," Trent said as he got us back onto the road and headed toward Grayson's house.

Five minutes later he pulled to a stop in front of the driveway. "Do you want me to come in with you?"

He was asking because of the yelling I could hear even within the car. I couldn't make out what Nigel and Grayson were talking about, but maybe he could. "I'll just go in and get a few things. I was just going to get my car, but I think it would be best if I got the rest of my stuff right now too."

"I could come in and make sure you're safe while you get them," he offered again.

And then I realized what he was really saying. "Grayson isn't going to hurt me." I was absolutely sure about that. "And this isn't a domestic violence issue either. His friend was an ass to me so I left."

"And what did Grayson do?"

I turned and glared up at the house, where I could see Nigel and Grayson walking back and forth behind the curtains. With the light from the living room shining out, I could clearly make out their silhouette.

"If he'd said anything, I wouldn't have left. That was the problem." I opened up the door and started to get out, but I swung my attention back to Trent. "Thanks for the ride. And the talk."

Trent rolled his hands over the steering wheel. "Is there anything I can do to make it up to you?"

He didn't need to do anything for me. I'd already gotten over it, and it had been years ago. I felt better now that he knew everything, but it wasn't like it was a new memory or even like I'd opened up some old wound. That night with him had just been the start of the nights I'd had with guys from the app. There'd been some sexual freedom in it, at first, but now I just felt wrong and empty.

"Treat Caleb right," I finally decided to say.

"Sure. I like to think that I do. He married me, so I must have been doing something right."

I rolled my eyes and got out of the car. Going up to Grayson's front door was difficult, but the yelling stopped as soon as I came in. Grayson grabbed me in a hug before I could even close the front door.

"Hi." I patted him awkwardly on his back.

"When you left I was worried about you." He released me and stepped back.

I put some more distance between us too, which backed me up against the island. "I was fine. I went to go hang out with a horse for a while. And right now I'm just back to get my things, and then I'm going."

His eyes got wide. Nigel was apparently forgotten as Grayson stepped close again and rested his hands on my chest and then my hips. "Please don't leave. We'll talk. Nigel will apologize for what he said."

Nigel snorted from across the room, and I moved out of Grayson's hold to be able to see his friend better. "So? What's the issue? I'm too young, too stupid, too what?"

Nigel sneered at me. "All those things and so much more. You're screwing Grayson Pendleton, of the Virginia Pendletons, which is fine when you were just someone he shared hotel rooms with. But now you're here, living in his house, and he's calling you his boyfriend? What game do you think you're playing at? It's gold-digging little sluts like you that ruin perfectly good men."

Grayson stepped up beside me and rested his hand on my lower back. "Nigel, that's enough. I've already asked you to leave a few times now. I'd really like you to go."

If he wasn't leaving by now, I didn't know why Grayson kept bothering. Clearly Nigel thought what other people wanted wasn't of any importance to him. I was glad that Grayson was trying to stick up for me, but really it didn't seem to be doing much good at this point.

"What I'm playing at, is that I like him too. He's a friend. I wouldn't call him my boyfriend, and it's not like we're sharing a room. We're just two people who were living together up until tonight, and most of that time, he wasn't even in town." I took a deep breath, because there was more and this part I needed

Grayson to understand. So I turned and gave my attention fully to him. "I'm not out for your money. I don't even care that you have any. You could be as broke as me and I'd be completely fine with that. But what you did tonight, how you didn't stick up for me before, that wasn't okay. And that's why I'm leaving."

I headed upstairs and started gathering my stuff together. There was more yelling, then the front door slammed. A few minutes later, Grayson came up to the bedroom he'd given me. It wasn't my room, but I had started to think of it like that in the days since I'd brought my stuff into it. But now it was just a room I'd been occupying for the past few days. It was stupid, but I felt bad that I hadn't washed the sheets. I'd meant to, but I'd also meant to leave when I was much calmer too if I didn't stay for the full month.

"I don't want you going back there," Grayson said from the doorway as I finished stuffing my dirty clothes into my bag. I'd meant to do laundry too at some point.

I didn't turn to look at him. "I don't want to stay with someone who won't even defend me when their friend is being a jerk to my face."

He came forward and rested his hand on my shoulder. I didn't shake him off. I didn't finish packing either. I just knelt there under his hand and wished I didn't feel like I was so angry I could cry.

"I know. I'm sorry. But I don't want you going back to your apartment, where you're not safe. I'll go to a hotel tonight. I'll be out of the state again in a week anyway. And then when I get back, we'll talk again."

I sighed and got to my feet. I didn't want to go back to my apartment, and Brent, but I didn't think that it was right that Grayson be forced to stay at a hotel when he had his own house just because he was worried about me.

"Compromise. I stay, you leave me alone, we'll talk later?" He smiled at me and tried to kiss me, but I pulled away from him. "I'm not done being mad at you."

"Of course not. Nor should you be." He took a few steps back. "If you need anything…."

I nodded. I knew where he was. But I really didn't want to be around him right then. "See you later."

"Good night." He left, and I dumped all of my stuff back out in the middle of the room. Then I kicked off my sneakers before lying down on the bed. It wasn't even six o'clock, and I already knew that the next few hours until I was tired enough to go to sleep were going to be miserable.

CHAPTER TWELVE

Grayson

I RARELY baked. It was too much effort just for one person. But when I came back downstairs and realized my grand dinner plans were ruined, and also that I'd possibly lost Eli permanently this time, I decided to try my hand at cookies. Chocolate chip cookies to be exact. The first batch came out horribly, as did the second. I was surprised that I even had all the ingredients to make cookies in the first place. They'd been hidden in the coat closet for some reason, and I didn't remember putting them there. By the third it was nearly nine o'clock, and I was starving. But at least they came out nicer than the last two.

And they were the ones that brought Eli out of his room in search of food, so I couldn't discount them completely. I was sitting on the couch with a plate of cookies and a glass of milk on the table beside me when he joined me with his own plate and glass. He didn't say anything to me, just sat down on the other end of the couch and pulled his feet up under him. It was a chilly evening, and I'd brought one of my blankets down to wrap around my legs. I silently offered it to him as well, and just like that, we were sitting together under the blanket, eating cookies. I was careful not to touch him, in case he was still angry at me, but simply being near him felt like a blessing in and of itself.

After an hour of just sitting together and watching a movie I'd long forgotten about, he laid his head gently against my shoulder. I put my arm between his back and the couch and rested my hand on his hip to hold him close. I was so much bigger than him, but he still fit well against me.

"Do you really think of me as your boyfriend, or were you just saying that because calling me your fuck toy in public would be frowned upon?" he asked me a few minutes later.

I frowned. I wasn't really sure how to answer his question. "I never thought of you as just someone to have sex with. I always wanted to know who you were, but it seemed as if you would never let me close enough to find out, as if your body was the only thing you'd ever be comfortable sharing with someone else. So I took the only parts of you that you seemed willing to give. But I'm nearly fifty, and having a boyfriend doesn't seem like the right word for how I think about you. I care about you, and I want you to be safe. I like having you here, and while I'm not ready to have us share a room, I enjoy sharing my house with you." I took a chance and leaned over to kiss the top of his head. He didn't pull away from me, so I took that as a good sign. "What about you? How do you feel about me?"

"I realized tonight that I've never really tried to date. It was easier, somehow, to simply be the one who was used and live with that, as I assumed that all men only wanted that from me and somehow I was only ever worth what I could do in bed. But I like this, how we are right now. And I liked it when we ate ravioli together. I'd like to do more dating types of things with you. If that makes me your boyfriend, then that's fine by me. I'd prefer that to the title of fuck toy any day. But if you want me to be someone who is in your life and not just in your bed, I need you to not let Nigel talk to me like that again."

He was right. That wouldn't be happening again. "He isn't allowed back here. He's still my friend, and I'll have dinner with him on occasion, but having him here with you isn't going to happen until he learns to respect you."

"Thank you."

I nodded and rubbed my hand over his hip.

"Do you like traveling as much as you do? Wouldn't it be more fun not to have to go everywhere all the time?"

I chuckled. "It would be, but this is the life I've had for years. I don't know if I'd have any idea what to do with myself if I wasn't gone half the week. What would you want to do with me?"

I expected him to say something sexual to go with my teasing, but he simply shrugged. "I hear the fishing around here is pretty good. And we could go on walks through the woods."

Clearly he needed a push in the right direction. "We could wake up together some mornings."

"You could join me at the rescue sometimes. We have open houses once a quarter, and you could handle the bake sale portion. Or the grilling of the hot dogs. I always end up singed in some way from doing that. It never fails."

All right. I could take a hint. He settled farther back against me.

"I would like you to consider moving in with me. Permanently. You'd still have your room. But you would be here, and you'd be safe."

He sighed and pulled his knees up to his chest. "I'd rather that you want me here because you like my company and want me around, rather than being worried about what I'll do when I'm not here for you to supervise me. And, besides, don't forget. A few hours ago I was ready to walk away completely, so moving in fully and giving up my apartment isn't something that's going to happen right now. As much as I appreciate your offer and as much as you want me to jump right into being your live-in boyfriend."

He was right. Of course he was. But that didn't mean I had to like it.

"And, if you were my boyfriend and if we were living together full-time, I would want you home more than half the month."

That wasn't an unreasonable request at all, so I wasn't entirely sure why I suddenly felt the need to balk at the idea of changing my life so completely for him. It felt like if I did that now, it would be on a whim and not because I'd actually thought things through. But, as I thought about it, I realized I would like to have that added time with him.

"Stay here for a month, and if we still want to be together after that time, I would like you to give up your apartment and move in here with me, and at that time I will begin to scale back my clients so that I am only out of town a weekend per month at the most. Is that something that could work for you?"

He lay back on the couch, pushing the blanket off of himself. "I can live with that. So you have a month to prove to me that you can be a good boyfriend. And I'll have a month to figure out how to live with someone else and trust them."

I smiled at him and turned so that I was covering his body with mine. He opened his legs to me in a clear invitation, one I wanted to take him up on, but I'd realized something else too. In all the time we'd ever been together, I'd never once just taken care of his needs without any thought to my own. I wanted him, and having him pinned under me as I began gently kissing him was already making me hard. But for once I wanted to show him that I could do something just for him.

I pushed my hand between our bodies and pressed against his fly. He arched toward me and moaned deep in his throat, as if he was needy and desperate. I loved having him like that. When he came and his face lit up with pleasure a moment before he closed his eyes and his whole body shook with the vibrations of his orgasm, that was a beautiful sight. I'd seen some of the most beautiful things in the world. The Venus de Milo, the Mona Lisa, the Grand Canyon, but I'd never gone back to any of them. Seeing Eli's pleasure was addictive, and I needed more of it.

His pants were easy to get undone, and he reached for mine as well, but I brushed his hands away. "Tonight is for you," I explained as he looked up at me in confusion. Whether he believed me or not wasn't really the point right then. But I was pretty sure that, judging by his mistrustful expression, he thought I wouldn't be able to stick with that promise.

He was naked under his jeans, something I loved about him, and I gripped him tightly and began stroking him. I sucked on his neck and pushed his sweater up to expose his stomach. I ran my fingers lightly over that thin trail of hair that went from his navel to the base of his cock. With every long stroke of my fingers over his cock, he arched against me. His movements were erratic, fueled by his pleasure but lacking any real rhythm. I didn't mind.

I touched him with abandon, savoring his smooth skin and his lean muscles as he moved against me. He curled his fingers over my shoulders, and once or twice I thought I heard him gasping my name. Then there was that rush of pleasure and beauty that flushed his skin as he came off the couch and arched into my hand with his orgasm.

He lay panting and sweaty under me. I kissed his cheeks, his eyelids, his forehead, and then his lips before I started to move away from him to go wash off my hand. I'd managed to contain most of his come to my fingers so there was very little to do as far as cleaning him up if he wanted to stay right like that for a while. With his jeans unbuttoned and his sweater pushed up over his chest, I wouldn't have minded being able to look at him like that for a few more hours. But it was late, and I was sure he had to work at some point the next day.

As I was getting up, he reached for the button of my jeans again. But I pushed his hands away, just as I had when he'd tried to undo my pants before. "Eli, I said that tonight was for you."

He let his hands fall back to his stomach. He didn't seem concerned at all by his own nudity. "It doesn't have to be. You don't owe me this for failing to say something earlier."

Is that what he thought I was doing by giving him pleasure tonight? Mindful of his come on my hand and how I didn't want to make everything dirty, I leaned down to kiss him.

"I didn't do this because I felt that I needed to apologize to you some more. I wanted to make you come without any expectations of having to return the favor." I stood back up and headed to the kitchen sink. When I came back, he was dressed again and under the blanket, as he watched me.

"There's no such thing as one-way sex. Everything leads to more."

He sounded so sure of himself, like I was the one who didn't know how the world worked instead of the other way around. "With me, it doesn't always have to."

Eli frowned but said nothing more until it was time to go to bed. At that point I got up and headed upstairs.

"Good night," I told him. "I'll be here in the morning this time."

"I don't go to work until eleven. Maybe we can get breakfast at the diner."

I smiled at him. "I would like that very much."

"Me too."

Once I was safely in my room, I undressed and lay down naked on my bed. Just because I hadn't needed anything from Eli that night didn't mean that I hadn't been fighting back a hard-on, which had been nearly painful in my pants. I was so sensitive as the cool air brushed over me that I was sure it wouldn't take much to get me to come. I grabbed a shirt to have nearby and stroked myself with one hand as I cupped my sack with the other. I thought about Eli on his knees over me as he rode me like we so often did. He would toss his head back and slide his slick hole over my cock as he sought his pleasure before I took mine from him. I knew his whimpers and his soft cries. I could practically taste his skin against my tongue. He was always a bit salty, and he smelled clean, like he took care of himself despite the perpetual dirt under his nails.

Fucking him made me happy. Seeing him come and getting to see that sated smile on his face that was just for me made me nearly delirious with pleasure. That was why I always wanted him to come first, because getting to see him like that nearly took me over the edge every time.

I imagined our bodies slapping together as he rode me, and how he curled his fingers over my chest. Sometimes his short nails bit into the coarse curls on my chest. I'd thought to shave myself completely for him once, but then I'd remembered how much he seemed to like getting to touch my hairy chest and stomach, and I'd quickly abandoned that idea.

It was thinking about him bucking against my cock as he came that sent me over the edge as I jacked myself to the memories of our times together in so many different hotel rooms. I wanted him in my bed, just as I'd imagined him being. I wanted to fuck him so hard into the mattress that I was afraid my bed would break. But I also wanted to enjoy him slowly and really take my time with him as I listened to each distinct cry that came from his throat. I loved having him both ways, and any other way that I could get him too.

SOMETIME IN the middle of the night, he came into my room and joined me in my bed. He wasn't naked, but I was, and that must have surprised him because he hesitated against me. I took his hand and silently brought him closer to me until his back was against my chest. I'd been limp while asleep, but now with his ass pressed so perfectly against my cock, I was starting to wake up fully.

"You can if you want to. You know I won't say no to you."

His quiet voice, and the words he'd used, were an instant splash of ice water over my libido. I wanted him, but not like that. He'd come to share my bed, not my body.

I wrapped my arms around him and held him close. "Good night, Eli. I'll see you in the morning."

I imagined that he was smiling as he said good night to me too.

CHAPTER THIRTEEN

Eli

I WAS up at seven, and I crept quietly out of Grayson's bed and into the bathroom where I showered, which wasn't nearly as quiet as I'd hoped it would be. Grayson was up by the time I came back to his room a half hour later, with my hair still damp, but I was dressed. He wasn't yet, but he was getting his things together to get into the shower.

"Thank you for last night." It didn't matter which part I was talking about, either the hand job or the hours I'd spent sleeping peacefully in his arms.

"You're welcome."

I shifted my weight on the balls of my feet. "It's a new day. Does that mean we can start doing things to each other again?"

He chuckled. "Is that your not-so-subtle way of saying you're horny and want to have sex?"

I laughed. He had me there. "Yeah. Pretty much. So...."

Grayson smiled at me and put his things down on the dresser. "What would you like?"

I began stripping off my clothes. It didn't matter that I'd just showered. I could do that again. And we'd still have time for a quick breakfast before I had to get to the rescue to help work with some of the new horses Evaline had brought back from the kill auctions.

I wanted him, and I knew I'd enjoy it. "You to fuck me."

He shook his head and took my hand as he led me over to the bed. "It's a little early for fucking. How about I make love to you? Like I did the other time?"

I nodded. That would work for me too. I slipped out my plug, and he took care of himself with a condom and some lube as I lay down in the middle of the bed and waited for him. He slid inside easily, and I hissed as he stretched me. My legs went around his waist, and I laid my hands on his upper arms to hang onto him. This was all so familiar to me. His strokes were slow and deliberate. He'd be erratic later, but right now he was just getting started.

Grayson kissed me gently, everything about him seeming to want to be careful as he dipped his hips to stroke inside of me. I wasn't a fragile thing that he had to worry about breaking, and after our months of hardcore fucking in hotel rooms, I knew he understood that by now. But this early in the morning, he was right. I liked having him as I was this morning. This slow, sensual, deliberate way in which he wanted to take my body worked for me.

"I heard you last night," I told him softly as I ran my hands over his shoulders and down his chest.

He chuckled and sounded nervous while he did it. "What do you think you heard?"

If he wanted to play coy with me, I could beat him at his own game. I mimicked his voice and his volume as I said, "Oh Eli, yes, fuck yes, oh God, yes."

"I did not say all of that last night."

Yes, he did. But he probably didn't remember it. His grunts and moans were mostly unintelligible, but they still worked for me because I got the basic meaning behind them. He was enjoying his time with me and liked being inside of me. Coming from a guy as sweet as Grayson was, that was a pretty big compliment, I thought.

"What were you thinking about while you jacked off to me?"

"That makes it sound like an invasion. I didn't mean for you to hear me." He sped up and panted a bit. My head fell to the side, and I chewed on my bottom lip some as he started rubbing against my prostate. I wondered if I could come completely untouched by him that morning.

"It wasn't, though. I've jacked off thinking about you lots of times. Tell me what you were thinking about? Please?"

He groaned against my neck. It was a sound half of pleasure and half of frustration. But he did relent. "You on top of me. Riding me like you do before I flip you over and take you hard."

I loved those times when I lay there under him completely satisfied and he fucked me just like he wanted to. I was sometimes sore the next day, but it was so worth it in the moment while he was in me and taking me like that.

"Mmm. Yes. I like that too."

He kissed me, and I pressed myself up against him.

"I know you do. I don't think I've ever met someone who liked what I did as much as you do."

I smiled against his lip and wrapped my arm around his shoulders. "You know what else I like?"

"What?"

"When you come."

He took the hint. Sweet and slow was nice. But I was awake now, and we were running out of time. He needed to hurry if we wanted to have breakfast. And that meant I'd have to come without being touched another time because I didn't want to wait that long.

Only when I went to wrap my hand around my cock as I dug the fingers of my other into his shoulder, I felt him press tightly against my prostate, and I bit down on my bottom lip and waited, hoping that it would happen. I'd read about guys coming without having to be jacked off before, in guy magazines, but I thought it was all bullshit until Grayson slid against me repeatedly at just the right angle.

And then I was crying out and hanging on to him as my orgasm pushed through me and made my vision blur. I saw dots of light that faded quickly to gray, and I lost control of my own breathing for a few seconds as my pleasure burst out.

He rode my orgasm out, quickly gaining speed until he was thrusting into me as hard as he'd ever done, and the bed was bouncing under us. I was smiling, and I probably looked like a crazy person, but that didn't matter to me because I loved every second of being with him like this. Under him, on top of him, in front of him with my body pressed hard against the wall—it didn't matter. I loved it all from him. As long as he was in me and fucking me as hard as he could, it was the most wonderful thing I could imagine as far as sex went.

He came with a low groan against my collarbone and then collapsed on top of me. We both needed showers now, but it was totally worth it. Even though we did have to rush through breakfast so that I could still get to work on time that morning.

WHEN I got to the rescue, Mason was there waiting for me. He slung his arm around my shoulders, which was a bit hard for him since he was a good five inches shorter than me. Grayson was about six inches taller. Mason would have a really hard time doing that to him too. It would be nearly impossible. Thinking about Grayson made me smile. Weird.

"Hey," he said.

"Anything going on?" I asked him. There were more cars in the parking lot than there normally were.

Mason dropped his arm from around my shoulders as we headed into the office for me to sign in. "Don't know. Evaline said all hands on deck today."

That in itself was pretty unusual. I hurried over to the daily clipboard to sign in for work, and then Mason and I walked out to the big barn where everyone was hanging out. There were three barns, but only one that would fit us all. I had seniority, so I went to the front where Evaline was.

She hugged me, because she hugged everyone, and then I looked over her shoulder. In the barn, Thrall lay on his side. He was an ancient gelding who was at least thirty. And he'd been Evaline's first rescue.

I went into the stall before anyone could stop me. Only then did I realize he was already gone. There was nothing I could do for him. I just sat there against his side in the hay and stroked my hand down his leg. He was a thoroughbred, built for speed and grace, and he'd done well on the tracks until he hadn't. He was a descendant of Secretariat, not that who was in his lineage mattered as a rescue horse, but I had always thought it made him pretty cool.

"What happened?" I asked Evaline.

She shook her head and came into the stall with me. Others were crying. I hadn't noticed it before. But now that he knew, Mason looked pretty upset as well. Thrall had been a barn favorite. I held up my hand for him too, and he joined me. He had no concept of personal space as he came over and sat right down in my lap like a child. That got some looks from people, but I was too worried about Evaline to pay any attention to them.

She knelt down next to Thrall's beautiful black head and rubbed her hands over his face. "He just laid down in here while we were doing the morning feedings. He went quietly. We should be glad about that. Shouldn't we?"

I supposed that we could be. But I knew she was more upset about losing him. "You should take a few days off. I can handle the rescue. It's not a big deal." It was, a bit. I'd never had full control of it. But I didn't want her to have to worry about that while she mourned Thrall.

"I could?" She looked surprised.

"Of course. Tell me what you'd like done with him, and I'll take care of it."

Evaline gave me a shaky smile and got to her feet. "Thank you, Eli. I think that would be best. You're such a good boy. I think he would be best with the others. In the back pasture. You know where."

Of course I did. As a sanctuary, we had lots of older horses, and not all of them got adopted or fostered before their time was up. "He'll be taken care of."

She kissed my forehead, and I touched her callused, weathered hand, and then she was gone and getting into her truck. I got Mason off my lap, and then I stood up to address everyone.

"Evaline is going to take a few days off to mourn Thrall. He was the favorite for a lot of us, so if you'd like to take a day off too to mourn him, please sign out before you do. If you're here on community service and need me to talk to your officer so that you can take the day off, please let me know. Otherwise you all know what to do. The back pasture is off-limits today while I have people out here to help him."

A girl started sniffling, but a boy near her scoffed. I heard something about how she shouldn't cry over a horse, and then I was in front of him. He was at least three years older than me, and taller than Grayson, but I was in charge of the rescue right then, and I wouldn't tolerate that kind of crap.

"Leave. You're fired. Effective immediately."

"We're all volunteers. You can't fire us."

He was a community service worker, so I kind of could, actually. I stood my ground. "You're trespassing. Get off the sanctuary." I saw a few of his friends watching us with interest. "Take your friends and anyone else who doesn't respect or care about the horses with you. Evaline may have liked you, or thought that the sanctuary needed the extra hands, but you just pissed me off. We all loved Thrall. You don't get to treat other people, or the horses here, with such obvious disrespect. So, again, and for the last time, get off this sanctuary."

Mason came up behind me and bumped me on the back of my shoulder. He was so tiny that if it came to a fight, like I hoped it wouldn't, he wouldn't be much help at all. But I still appreciated his support anyway.

"Fuck you," the guy growled at me, before he started backing away from us. I snorted because there was no way that was ever going to happen. A few people left with him. I wasn't sad to see them go at all.

"Okay, everyone else, take some time to get yourselves together or have a day off. We'll be okay if you need to go home and take care of yourselves. You can go in and say goodbye to him too." I moved aside so that they could crowd in to touch the old gelding.

Mason followed me back into the office. "Ricky was such an asshole."

"Who?" I asked him as I looked through Evaline's list of phone contacts.

"The guy...."

"Oh." I hadn't really known him. Most of my work was off-site doing home assessments. "Okay, a few things to do today before we go check on the horses. You okay being my assistant for a bit?"

He sat down across from me while I called the burial company, who said that they would be out within a few hours and just to have the area between Thrall and the back pasture clear. They started to explain the process about how they were going to drag him out of the stall by his back hooves and then load him onto a flatbed truck, but really I didn't need the details. I'd seen enough horses buried to know what was going to happen without having to be told it all again. I thanked them for their speed, then got to the appointments.

"I need to move these assessments to next week. Can you call this one, and I'll call these two? Don't schedule me for more than one in a morning or an afternoon, please."

Mason got to it and so did I. That took a total of twenty minutes. I explained that I was very sorry that I needed to change the time of our appointments, but we had something come up at the rescue. The two families I talked to were both very understanding. Mason, though, was explaining everything to whoever he was talking to. I reached over and tapped his arm.

"It's my mom," he quickly explained. "I'm letting her know that I'll be late getting home tonight because you need me for some extra stuff."

"Oh. Okay." That was actually a good idea. I took out my phone and texted Grayson. *One of the favorite horses died. I gave Evaline a few days off to grieve. I'll be really late getting back. Looks like I'm running a rescue now.*

His reply came back a few minutes later while I was counting the number of volunteers who had signed in and those who had also signed out, and from that, I could decide how to get everything done that day. *Is there anything I can do?*

His attempt to help made me smile. *Not really. I'll try not to wake you if I'm getting in super late.*

Take care. With his last reply, I decided to go out to the barn and get to work. We all had a long day ahead of us, but at least most of the volunteers stayed late to help us get it all done. There were barns to clean out, I had to oversee Thrall's burial and write the guys a check from the sanctuary account. I was glad I had that kind of authority.

Yes, the circumstances of getting to run the rescue for a day sucked so hard. But at the same time, I liked the pressure of it. Evaline needed me, and I had nothing else to do but step up and take over where she'd left off. The only person waiting for me was Grayson, and he was an adult. He could handle some stuff on his own until things settled down there.

Unfortunately things didn't ever calm down. Not until after eight o'clock. Mason was passed out on the couch in the office, waiting on his mom to come get him. I was barely awake after working harder than I ever had at the rescue. I was sore and definitely exhausted too.

Then Grayson came into the office. I smiled up at him and realized how hungry I was the instant I smelled his Chinese food takeout.

"Hi," he said, a bit awkwardly as a bleary-eyed Mason started to sit up on the couch.

Mason was so unattractive as he smacked his lips together, then he realized we weren't alone. "Uh...."

"Mason, this is Grayson. And Grayson, this is *my* best friend right there." I hope he got my point. Mason was my Nigel. Only my best friend wasn't an asshole to people who he thought of as being beneath him.

Grayson put the food containers down on the desk and offered Mason his hand. "It's nice to meet you. I brought a lot of food. Would you like to join us?"

Mason looked to me, as if he needed my permission or something ridiculous like that, but I nodded and gave it to him anyway. Then he was diving into the food, and I was joining Grayson on the couch with a box of sweet and sour chicken in my hands. He had broccoli and beef. Mason grabbed the lemon chicken and found a place to sit at the desk. There were still two more containers of food that we hadn't opened.

"You got way too much food," I told Grayson as I leaned against his side and began eating my fried chicken. I didn't even care about the sauce. I just liked the simple things like juicy chicken in a light batter that made the whole headache of my day kind of fade into the background.

"I didn't know what you'd like," he explained.

"Thanks for bringing food. And sharing it with me." Mason spoke up from about four feet away from us.

I leaned my head against Grayson's shoulder. It made eating awkward, but I didn't have any sauce to accidentally spill on him, so that was okay. "Yeah, this was really nice." Actually, no one had ever done this for me. It made me warm and somehow sleepy. Like I could have fallen asleep right there while I leaned against his shoulder. I still had an hour to drive back to his house, so that probably wasn't a good thing.

"Mason, when is your mom supposed to pick you up?" I asked him.

He took out his phone and looked at it. "She won't get off work for another hour. I can just take the bus or something. That's my plan, anyway."

"I'll take you. No reason you should be here this late." I'd been doing paperwork, but he'd been resting. He was exhausted too. And now that I had food, I really didn't want to stay at the sanctuary anymore. I loved it there, but there came a point when doing the daily reports could wait, and I didn't exactly love paperwork to begin with.

I was nearly done with my food, but I didn't want to get up. I was far too comfortable right there. But as soon as I ate my last piece of chicken, I got up to toss out my container, and since Mason was done too, I took his as well. The next container I grabbed was honey walnut shrimp. It was sweet and creamy and tasted like dessert and shrimp put together. I loved it and savored every last bite. Mason started eating some kind of fried rice.

"Do you want to share mine?" I asked Grayson.

"Just one bite."

I could have let him take it himself. But feeding him from my little plastic spoon was much more fun. He smiled at me, and then I gave him a quick kiss before going back to my dinner. I caught Mason watching us, and he looked so absolutely wistful and lost that I had to laugh at him.

"Your time is coming," I told him.

"I wish. I'm going to be alone forever."

I snorted and finished up my dinner. I was full and barely awake by the time I was done with the second box of food. Mason didn't look too much better off than I did. "I should get him home," I told Grayson. "So I'll see you back at the house?"

"Why don't I drive you two? I'll bring you back here tomorrow when you come back for work, and that way I don't have to worry about you driving in the mountains when you're this tired."

Thornwood really wasn't in the mountains. Or if it was, it was just barely there. But I saw his point. "You wouldn't mind?"

He shook his head, and a few minutes later, we were in his luxury car, which I was too tired to notice the details of more than that I was sitting in a leather seat and his display had navigation. I didn't even have a display. Mason was passed out in the back within a few minutes.

"It's okay, I know where he lives."

Grayson nodded and started following my directions to get Mason back to his mom's house in Highlands Ranch. "You two seem close."

"We are. We've also never had sex, if that's what you were trying to get at."

"You got me. I was wondering about that."

I smiled over at him and sleepily offered him my hand. He took it, and we held hands for the whole twenty minutes it took to get Mason home.

"Where do you live?" Grayson asked me after we'd dropped Mason off and made sure that he'd been able to get inside his house, before Grayson got us back on 470.

"Castle Rock."

He turned around to head south.

"What are you doing?" I asked him. I was starting to become more awake.

"Taking you to your apartment so that you can get a few things. No reason you should continue to wear the same few outfits. And I don't mind taking you."

While he was being very sweet, I really hoped that Brent wasn't watching my apartment like it seemed he had been so that he could come over. I really didn't want there to be any trouble. I hadn't heard from him at all, which was great, but I didn't expect that to last forever.

"Are you okay after the horse died?" he asked me after I finished giving him directions.

"I'm a bit sad, and I really liked him, but after my dad, I kind of got over my shock about death. I mean, I was seven, and my dad was dead. I don't have those kinds of shocked feelings that people told me about today. Does that make me cold and heartless?" I'd been thinking about that today, while everyone had been crying and I'd been trying to figure out how we were going to take care of all the horses with so many less people to help out. We'd made it work, but it had still been a lot harder than I'd anticipated to get everything done today with no one really being focused and being shorthanded anyway. I was glad the assholes were gone, of course I was, but I'd needed a lot of help too.

"No. I think it actually makes you practical."

I hadn't thought of it like that, but maybe he was right. "So…." I needed a change of topic away from my day, though it was a nice surprise to have someone even asking about it and how I was doing with the stress and losing Thrall. Usually people just didn't bother to see how anyone else was doing these days. And if they did ask, then it wasn't like they cared to know. It was just about making polite conversation. But Grayson actually wanted to know, which was nice, and it made me feel special. "So you're from Virginia? Or at least your family is?"

He chuckled. "Yes. They are. But I'm not close to the Virginia Pendletons anymore, as Nigel called me. He makes a big deal about my family history and their name and place in that society. I don't value it at all."

That surprised me. I knew he had money, and I just thought it came with some kind of a title and land and maybe a fucking castle or something the way Nigel had made it sound like such a big deal that Grayson was part of *the* Virginia Pendletons. Like wow, let me bow down and kiss his boots or some shit like that. But Grayson was cool with it.

"Are you still close with your family?"

"Not at all."

He didn't seem put out by that, which made me think that it had been a long time since he'd spoken to them. "Because they got upset at you when you came out?"

This time he laughed. "Actually, I didn't get that chance. I told my father that I was going to be getting a business degree, instead of studying medicine like he did or law like my mother did, and that was the end of it. I didn't realize that I was only interested in men until I was in college, and by then they'd cut me out of their lives completely."

I snorted. "Because you wanted to do something besides what they wanted?"

"They more or less took it as me turning my back on the family name and everything they'd given me. They didn't take it well. I was surprised he'd left me this house at all."

We arrived at my apartment complex, and I gave him further directions to get him to my specific building. "Do you want to wait out here, or would you like to come in?"

"Are you uncomfortable with me seeing your place?"

"I'm not. And I'm not ashamed of it either. My furniture is crap, but it's functional, and you've seen how I dress. I know they aren't your standards, but I like my way."

He smiled at me and rubbed his thumb over the back of his knuckles. "I think that's one of the things I like most about you."

"What is?"

"That you make no apologies for who you are or what you like."

I blushed as I smiled back at him. And, after he'd parked in front of my building, he leaned over to kiss me. I didn't even mind getting kissed by him in front of the place I lived. He was older than me by a lot, and probably many people would think he was my sugar daddy, but I knew better. And if anyone had a problem with it, then that had nothing to do with me or him or us. As a couple. I swallowed as I pulled back. I'd just thought of us as a couple. Holy shit. Okay, I could handle that.

"Are you sure you don't mind me coming in? You look upset by something."

I was quick to shake my head. "I'm freaking out over something, but it's not about you seeing my crappy apartment."

"Will you tell me what it is?"

I rolled my head to the side so that I could look at him. "Are we dating? Because that's what it feels like to me here. Only, I've never dated, so I can't be sure. But it doesn't feel like we're just hanging out and having sex. Want to fill me in?"

Grayson leaned forward and kissed my neck, and at the same time, he slid his hand between my legs and lightly gripped my inner thigh. He was teasing me, even as I opened my legs up wider for him so that if he wanted to touch me, he could. I'd never even made out with anyone in front of my apartment, but if he asked me to go down on him right there in the parking lot, I would without giving it a second thought.

"We are dating," he said, his warm breath skating across my neck. "And I will still have you naked whenever you let me."

I smiled and leaned my head back in the seat as he shifted and began roughly massaging my cock through my jeans. I was exhausted, but I wasn't so tired that I'd fall asleep on him if he wanted me. Which I really hoped he did, because as much as I liked that he'd just given me pleasure the night before, I'd really liked that morning when he'd pounded into me.

"Get inside. The faster I can have you naked, the happier I'll be."

"Sounds good." I got out of his car in a hurry and realized there was nothing I could do to hide my erection. I was thick and hard, and since I had on my riding pants, that was obvious. Grayson didn't miss it either, judging by his grin as he followed me along the sidewalk to my front door. Which had an eviction notice on it. I read it, briefly. I was to pay my back rent, plus a late fee, or I could move out.

I shrugged and tossed it in the trash as soon as I was in my place. "Guess trading sex for rent doesn't apply when I haven't been here in almost a week."

Grayson just shook his head, and I could tell he was angry, but I couldn't really bring myself to be. I'd expected this, in a way, because Brent had been pretty clear about what he'd wanted, and I hadn't been around in a few days for him to screw with.

"I hope I never meet him," Grayson said as he started looking at all my pictures of the horses on my walls.

I snorted and headed into my bedroom to pack up the rest of my clothes and the few things I didn't want Brent and his family put out at the dumpster. "Me too," I called back to Grayson as I went through my shirts. Most of them were polo shirts with the rescue logo on them. And all of my pants were jeans that I could comfortably ride in. The fact that my life was pretty much all about the rescue made me smile.

"Are these all horses at the rescue?"

I finished packing one bag and started with the next. "Yeah. But they're also all horses I either helped rescue or get adopted into new homes."

I came out of my bedroom to see him still staring at the pictures. I was nearly done packing.

"Will you tell me about each of them someday?"

"Sure. If you want to hear their stories. Most of them are pretty standard and boring, though. Teenager got a horse, teenager went to college, family didn't want to take care of the horse anymore, they brought the horse to the sanctuary, and we adopted it out."

Grayson smiled over at me, and I went into the kitchen to start bagging up the groceries I still had. I wouldn't be taking them to his house, but my neighbor was struggling, and she had a few kids. I didn't have much to give her, but I figured if she wanted it, she could use it. I wanted to leave a note with the groceries to let her know that if she wanted anything out of my apartment she could take it. I wouldn't be back there ever again.

And knowing that didn't make me sad at all. I wouldn't miss this apartment. It had just been a place for me to live, and once Brent had entered the picture, it had been pretty hellish for me.

"Can you take the pictures off the walls?" They were pretty much the only things I really wanted out of my apartment. I mean, my clothes were important to me too, and I liked them all, but they could be replaced. Some of the horses whose pictures I had hanging on my wall weren't living anymore. Evaline had their official photos still in their folders at the rescue, but these were the pictures of them that I'd taken.

While Grayson took care of my pictures, I went next door with a note and a bunch of groceries for my neighbor. Then I was ready to load up my stuff into the back of his car. In total it took us about half an hour from the time we arrived to when we were back on the road with the rest of my things.

"I'm glad you've decided to stay with me for the next month."

I sank into his leather seat. He turned on the heat, and I sighed blissfully. I could get used to riding around in his car. "Me too. I like living with you."

He reached over to touch my thigh, and I smiled. I must have drifted off, though, because the next thing I knew, I was being helped out of his car and stumbling groggily up to my bedroom in his house.

CHAPTER FOURTEEN

Grayson

ELI BARELY had time for coffee the next morning before he had to head down to Parker. I wanted to stay there with him, but I had things to do too.

"I'll try to get off in time to have dinner with you," he promised me before he got out of my car. We kissed briefly, and then he was gone.

I made reservations, but he couldn't make them. He texted me at six saying, *Just got a new rescue and need to get her processed. I'll be late. I'm sorry.*

I was disappointed, but I respected what he was doing more than I did with many other people's professions. He was out there helping. And my profession largely worked around restructuring companies, which often led to people losing their jobs.

As I sat there alone that night, eating delivery Thai food and thinking about his job versus mine, I began to question my profession entirely. Sure, I helped companies, but to make them more profits and lose those employees who worked against that goal. Thinking about the kind of pleasure, the fulfillment Eli probably got from his life made me wonder what I would have done had I not gotten into Yale. I doubted that I'd be doing anything worthwhile, and I wouldn't have even a fraction of the possessions that I did now, but how much of that actually mattered?

I was still thinking about it at quarter after eight when Eli came through the front door.

He looked beat, but he was smiling. "Hey."

I got off the couch and went to give him a hug. I was gentle with him, in case he'd been thrown by yet another horse, but he squeezed me back, showing me that he wasn't as fragile as I wanted to treat him.

"I missed you," I said into his sweaty hair.

"Missed you too."

He smelled like hay and leather and the unmistakable smell of horses. I didn't want to let him go, but I was sure he was hungry. "There's Thai food in the fridge."

He chuckled and moved out of my arms. I was reluctant to release him, and so I followed him into the kitchen, where he started dishing up some pad Thai. "We've got to get some food here soon."

Maybe. "I don't really like cooking just for myself. The cookies were an exception that won't be happening all that often, so don't start expecting them." At my mention of the cookies, he grabbed one out of the plastic bag they'd been stuffed into on the island.

He leaned over the island as we waited for his food to heat up in the microwave. "As soon as Evaline gets back to the sanctuary, I'll make us some dinner. Real dinner too, not popcorn or cereal." Eli didn't look as if he was joking even a little bit.

"You're serious. Aren't you? You've had cereal for dinner before? You said that before, but I thought you were joking at the time."

Eli grabbed his plate out of the microwave. "Of course. It's an easy, cheap meal. Though by your look of horror, I'm assuming you haven't."

"No, I haven't." He grinned at me, and I smiled right back. "If you had gone to college, what would you have done?"

He dug into his dinner. "Something with animals probably. I like them a lot more than most people. They never lie or slack off to go text their friends when I'm trying to unload hay with them. Like I was today." Eli rolled his shoulders. "I need to do an open house soon to get some more volunteers."

I'd wanted to make money and get my independence when I'd left for college. Eli just wanted to help animals. I came around the island to kiss him on his shoulder. He smiled and kept eating, but I did catch his blush.

"Would you have had your own horse rescue if you could have?"

Eli shook his head, which surprised me. "I like working at Green Acres, and I love what I do, but I know how hard Evaline worked to get it to where it is. Plenty of rescues, even dog and cat rescues, die off in their first year. Whenever she's ready to retire, I'll take it over, but I don't want to start my own. Why are you asking?"

"Just making conversation." While that was true, it was more than that for me. "I was thinking about my job compared to yours."

"You get to travel and don't get kicked by horses," he pointed out as he slurped up his noodles.

That was true. "Yes, but you're outside all the time. And what you're doing matters."

I loved that Eli didn't even try to lie and placate me by telling me that my job mattered too. "You want to come work at the rescue for a bit?"

I was pretty sure he was joking, but I wasn't as I slowly nodded. "Maybe. I was thinking about it today. How I envy you in that you do something you love and what you do makes a difference to someone."

"To the horses for sure."

"Yes, but also the people who get to adopt horses from you. I'd like to help somehow."

He smiled over at me. "That would be great. I'd really like that. Then I could be your boss and write you up for being lazy, if you ever were."

I kissed him on his hair again. "We'll see. Do you have to be back early tomorrow?"

I was sure that he would have to be, but then Eli shook his head. "Evaline is coming back tomorrow morning. She's still sad about Thrall dying, but she told me that after being at the sanctuary daily for the last twenty years, it's hard for her to take even a day off. So I'm off tomorrow. She said I deserved a break."

"There's a classic horror movie marathon on tonight...."

His expression went from exhausted and barely functioning to fully attentive in mere seconds. "Really...?"

I'd had a feeling he'd be excited about that. I was just glad we could enjoy it together, though I would have recorded it so we could watch it together another time. "Yes."

He rushed through his dinner, and minutes later we were curled up on the couch together with the blanket wrapped around us and him cuddled into my side. He didn't stay upright for long, though, because halfway through the first movie, which was about a mummy who had come alive in New York City in the fifties, he was already lying down with his head on my thigh. I rubbed his back idly as I thought about what I wanted to do with my life. I was happy with my career. Wasn't I? I had thought that I was. What would I do instead? I could volunteer for a few hours at the rescue, but that wasn't exactly a career. I wanted more, and I wanted what I did to matter.

I was nearly fifty and having a midlife crisis all because I was jealous of my twenty-five-year-old boyfriend and his life in which he made a difference and what he did mattered. I wasn't willing to give up my car or my things to live a simpler life like he did, but I did want to go to work and not think about the people

I would advise be fired after I left. I wasn't directly responsible for those people losing their jobs, but I was a big part of it, and I didn't know if I could be as detached as I had always been before. I wanted more out of my life and for myself, but I wasn't sure how to get it now so late in my life.

I needed something else to focus on, and Eli made a nice distraction. His hair was messy, and he hadn't changed out of his work clothes. He'd taken off his boots, but his boot socks were still on. He looked happy and exhausted. I thought he was absolutely stunning.

"You're staring," he said, but he was smiling.

I chuckled and ran my fingers through his hair. "I can't help it. What does the rescue lack most?"

"Money," he said automatically. "All charities need money constantly."

I had assumed that much. "What else?"

He frowned as he thought of an answer. "Um… hay, more volunteers, medicated grain for the older horses, more adopters, more fosters, a trainer who does everything and does a great job and doesn't charge anything for their services, a vet who works for free, a farrier too…."

"I get it," I told him. And I did. But I felt even more lost than before.

"Why are you asking?"

I shrugged and decided to be completely honest with him. "I wish I was doing something that made a difference. Like you do."

Eli rolled over onto his stomach and then sat up so that he could kneel next to me. "I got lucky with Green Acres. I was pretty lost before Evaline kind of found me. You could try volunteering for a few hours at the rescue. That way you're helping and you're still working."

I ran my hand up his arm. His muscles were tight, as if he was tense about something. I hoped that it wasn't the idea of me volunteering where he worked. I didn't want to push him into something he wasn't okay with.

"I don't need to be working as hard as I am, especially now that I don't have a mortgage. And I would like to do something helpful. I'm not sure what, but I'll spend some time and think about it. Would you mind me being at Green Acres?"

His answer was an immediate shake of his head, which made me happy. "But I can't give you any special attention or anything like that, and if you screw up, I'll still call you out on it. But I really would like the help. I had to throw out a bunch of people yesterday, and so we were really short yesterday and today."

"But Evaline doesn't need you back tomorrow? And why did you have to get rid of them?"

Eli pressed his forehead against my shoulder as if he was too tired to keep himself upright even to kneel next to me. I put my arm around his back, and with some maneuvering, we got him sitting on my lap and leaning against my chest. I liked him there where I could feel the warmth of him going from my neck, where he rested his head, to my thighs. He seemed comfortable too as he settled in nearly immediately. Or maybe he was just too tired to try to find a more comfortable position.

"She doesn't, and she let some of them back when they begged. I kicked them out because they didn't care about the horses. But they're on their second strikes, so the next time they screw up, they're gone for good and no amount of being nice to a sweet elderly lady is going to fix that."

He sounded rueful but also incredibly tired. "Would you like me to record the rest of these movies for us to watch later, and then we can go to bed?"

Eli tilted his head back to look up at me. "I'm not exactly sex material right now, but if you want me on my back, I'd be able to stay awake for that."

I kissed him gently and wished he hadn't taken that from what I'd said. I would always want him, but I didn't need him right that moment. "I wasn't asking you to come to bed for sex. I was saying let's get you to bed because you look like you're about to fall over and, while I might be able to carry you a short distance, I don't want to test that theory on the stairs and risk both of us breaking our necks when we inevitably fall in the process."

He laughed and gave me a nod. Minutes later the recording was set and he was walking upstairs as I trailed along behind him. He went into his room, and I wasn't disappointed. Having him in bed with me for one night didn't mean I would automatically assume he'd always be there. Even now that we were dating, I had no intention of insisting he give up his own space. We were living together, he was safely away from everyone else who had ever wanted to use him, and that was enough for me.

But ten minutes after I'd settled into my bed, he came through my open bedroom door. He'd showered and changed. "Is it okay if I sleep in here even though we won't be having sex?"

I moved over to the other side of the bed, instead of in the middle where I'd been sprawled, to give him some more room. "Of course it is. You're always welcome in here."

"I want you to know, though, that I'm not moving into your room. I still need my own. Even though this is my second night in here."

He was surprisingly articulate for someone as tired as he looked. I patted the bed beside me, urging him to get under the covers, which he did, but he was a bit stiff about it as if he was slightly uncomfortable.

I kissed the back of his neck, then his shoulders, as I came up behind him and pressed myself against the warmth of his shower-heated body. "I don't expect you to be in here every night," I told him. And each of my words seemed to ease him a little bit as I felt the tension drain out of him as he began to relax against me. "I know you still want your own room. I insist on it. I like having my space too. But that doesn't mean I'll ever turn you away when you come to me."

He breathed deeply and let his breath out on a sigh. He seemed relieved by my words and the promise in them. "Is it okay if we only ever share your bed? That way if I don't come to you, then you know I want to sleep by myself and just be alone for the night?"

I couldn't imagine what would make him not want to be near me, but I nodded anyway. Maybe he was thinking ahead to the eventual reality of when we would argue at some point and he might want to be alone. The other option was one that I instantly hated.

"As long as you don't have someone else in your bed with you."

"I may never have dated anyone before you, but I do understand the concept of commitment. I'm monogamous. I hope you are too."

I smiled against his damp hair, which smelled like my sandalwood shampoo. That one small detail made me happier than I could have imagined. "I am. I deleted the app this afternoon."

"I'll get rid of it in the morning." He sighed and sounded as if he was barely holding on to staying awake at this point. I knew he wouldn't last much longer before he was completely asleep, which was good because I was closing in on unconsciousness as well. "It'll be nice. Not to have it, I mean. To know that if I want to have sex with someone, you're right here. And I trust you. You don't hurt me."

I squeezed him close and hated that his definition of a good person to be with seemed to hinge on someone who didn't hurt him. There was so much else to consider, but he'd been through so many people who had left a negative impact on his life that I wasn't surprised by his words in the least. I was saddened by them, though.

I kissed his neck again. "I won't ever hurt you."

"You don't know that. You could get really mad and say something you don't mean one day."

He was right. I could. So I amended what I'd promised him. "I won't ever physically hurt you, and if I say something mean, I won't ever actually intend to say it."

"That's better. Night, Grayson."

I smiled at the back of his head. "Good night, Eli. Sleep well." He was snoring lightly within a few minutes, and I was quick to join him.

CHAPTER FIFTEEN

Eli

WE HAD breakfast at the diner the next morning, then went for a walk around the woods of Thornwood. It was all government land, so it wasn't like we were trespassing at all. As we walked between the trees, with my hand in his, I was instantly jealous of Caleb and how he got to ride horses through such a beautiful place every day. When I rode it was for work; I hadn't taken a horse out for a pleasure ride in years. There was always a purpose to it whether I was doing some training, evaluating a new rescue, or exercising a horse that hadn't been ridden in a while. I never left the arena, and I was always on a schedule. It must have been really nice for him to be able to just go out and decide to explore the woods for a while.

"I set up a meeting with Evaline for tomorrow morning while you were still asleep. Then I'll be gone from tomorrow afternoon until Saturday."

My expression must have fallen instantly with my dislike of the idea of him being gone because he laughed and tacked on, "It'll only be for two days."

I nodded, but I still didn't like it. "I know. I wish you didn't have to go, though. What do you even do while you're gone, anyway?"

He helped me around a thick tree root that I was ready to trip over. "I mostly fire people, or rather get them fired."

I didn't really know what to say to that, at least something that wouldn't sound horribly judgmental, so I kept my mouth shut.

"But I want to do something different. You've inspired me to want to move in a new direction."

I nearly did fall right then. I'd never inspired anyone before. It was a big word and a bigger feeling, and I didn't know what to do with it because when Grayson looked at me right then, I thought I could practically see how much he cared about me, and maybe even loved me, so clearly on his face. I wanted to run, but I also wanted to stay, and I didn't know what to do because I suddenly felt as if I was suffocating under the weight of how much he cared about me. I plopped to the ground on my ass and needed to breathe for a few seconds, so I put my head between my knees, because that's what everyone says to do, and I gasped deep gulps of air into my lungs.

Grayson went to his knees beside me and rubbed my back. "Eli? What's wrong?"

As soon as I was able to breathe normally again, I looked over at him. "Do you love me?"

He was quiet for a long moment as he just stared at me. Then he nodded, and his hand went still on my back. "I do."

I turned toward him so that I was sitting directly in front of him. I took his hand in mine, and I stared at it as I wondered what, exactly, I was supposed to say to that. "No one has ever loved me before."

"Is that why you just went into a panic? Because you figured out that I love you before I was ready to tell you?"

He sounded annoyed, and I smiled warily up at him. "Yes? A bit. That sounds really bad, though, so just pretend I saw a rattlesnake or something instead. I just... I don't know. It's so big."

"What is?" Grayson looked genuinely confused.

I thought the answer was obvious. "Being loved. It's huge. It's wanting to spend every day together. It's being happy that the other person is around. It's being sad when you're gone. It's missing you all the time when I have to work. It's overwhelming at times. Like I'm losing parts of me that are being taken over by wanting to be with you."

He pushed me back onto the moss and fallen leaves, and I didn't fight him at all as he lay over me and pinned me to the ground with his weight. "Are you saying that you love me too?"

Maybe I was. I nodded, though I was terrified to say the words. He kissed me gently, and I lay limp under him. Love was giving up something. Wasn't it? It meant no longer caring about anything else but that person. It meant that nothing else mattered. And I wasn't ready to give up everything that I cared about. I didn't want to stop caring about Mason, and I needed to work at the rescue. I wasn't ready to give my life over to Grayson and never have anything else.

"What's wrong?" he asked me, probably because I hadn't been kissing him back.

I didn't know how to explain everything that I was feeling to him. It sounded like madness inside my head when I thought about it, but he seemed perfectly rational and calm. "I can't give up everything right now. I'm sorry."

Grayson frowned down at me. "Give up what? I have no idea what you're talking about."

"When people fall in love, they stop caring about other things…." I said the words slowly as if I was talking to a child because Grayson clearly didn't seem to understand what I was saying. Maybe he hadn't figured out that part of love yet, and that's why he was so ready to rush into it. Or maybe he was at the stage in his life where not being who he was five minutes ago was okay with him. He did talk about wanting to change his life, so I figured that was probably it.

He was no longer looking confused now. Now he just looked sad as he stared down at me. "I'm going to take a guess and say that after your father died, your mom became all about whoever came into her life next?"

I nodded. That's what love was. That's what people did. She said that she was in love with the men that she was with, and that's why we couldn't do things together anymore.

"Were you neglected after that?" Grayson asked me.

I had to think about that for a while. I'd been making my own meals for a while at that point, and I'd always gotten myself ready for school on my own ever since first grade when I'd been told to do it myself. I didn't have an honest answer, not one that was clear anyway.

"I don't know. I had food. I had money to go get clothes when I needed them."

"But you weren't loved." Grayson filled in the gaps for me.

I hadn't been. My mother had been all about my father, and he'd been all about his drugs. There was no room for me in that world, even after my dad's death. She'd latched onto the next person who was willing to pay attention to her, and I was left in the background.

"No wonder you have such a misconception about what it means to be in love and to even feel love." He sounded sad, like he was close to pitying me.

"I don't want your pity," I told him, but my voice was a weak whisper instead of the snap I'd meant to bring into it.

He leaned down and kissed me again, and this time I kissed him back gently. He didn't put his tongue between my lips, only brushed his mouth over mine in a kiss that left me warm and knowing that he cared about me.

"I'm not pitying you, Eli. I'm admiring your strength and your resilience. What you're describing, that's not love. That's obsession and probably a lot of codependency. When I tell you I love you, it means I enjoy the times we spend together. But it's healthy to want time apart too. I haven't stopped being friends with Nigel, and I'm still doing my job. I haven't lost anything by loving you. I haven't given anything up. I've gained you in my life. And if you started leaving things behind in your own life to be with me, I'd be disappointed in your choices. Do you understand what I'm saying?"

I was trying to, but this was years of my thoughts that he was trying to get through. "Maybe. A bit. I'm sorry."

He smiled down at me. "Don't be. I want you to talk to me if the idea of us being in love ever makes you scared or anxious. Can you do that for me? Please?"

I could easily agree to that. Talking to him was one of the things I liked most about when we were together.

"Good." He slid off of me, and I sat up too. He offered me his hand, and we were back to walking through the woods after that. I figured he had to think I was crazy by now, if he hadn't already come to that conclusion on his own. But he didn't seem to think so. Instead it was as if he couldn't stop touching me. He kept brushing his fingers over my hand or reaching out to rub my shoulder or run his hand down my spine. I liked all of his touches and didn't shy away from a single one of them. I took his hand as we walked, and with the quiet of the forest around us and my racing heart slowing down and back to normal after my bout of panic, I felt as though I was coming close to something that might have been like peace.

CHAPTER SIXTEEN

Grayson

THE NEXT morning we drove in different cars even though we were both going to the rescue. I had to leave shortly after my meeting with Evaline, and Eli would be there until late. Once we got there, and I pulled in next to his beat-up old car, we got out and I went to him. The hour I'd spent driving close to him on the highway had been far too long for him to be apart from me. I'd had no idea that letting him know how much I cared about him would make me hate being apart from him.

I hugged him when he was barely out of his car. He melted against me, and I smiled into his hair. I loved that he didn't move away from me even though there were a few people who could see us, one of them being his friend Mason, who waved at me.

I kissed Eli, briefly, to keep even a hint of professionalism between us while we were both working. I didn't want there to be any problems for him because of my need to be close to him. He stayed in my arms even after the kiss, just standing there with his head on my chest as a cool breeze blew through the parking lot.

"I should get to work," he said after a few minutes in which we'd been silent.

I was probably already late. But I didn't want to let him go. "I'll say goodbye to you after my meeting. And it'll only be a few days that I'll be in Boston anyway."

He pulled back and smiled up at me. "I think it's funny that we used to go weeks apart and you didn't even know my name and we were fine. Now five minutes seems to be too much time away from you. It's kind of terrifying."

I chuckled and cupped his face as I kissed him again. "I guess it is. I'll see you soon." He nodded, and I stepped back this time. I took his hand, and we went into the office. I didn't know what he needed to do, but I was there to meet with Evaline. She got up from the desk and kissed my cheek as Eli bent over a clipboard on the desk. I watched him curiously until I realized he was just signing into work.

"Here you go, honey," Evaline said as she handed Eli a handwritten list of tasks. He had six things to do, which might not have been too many, except that I had no idea how long something like *Get Topaz to lift up her feet for grooming* would take him.

"Cool. See you in a few hours for lunch." He met my gaze, and I wasn't sure what would be appropriate to say in front of his boss. "Come see me before you go?"

"I already promised I would. If I can't find you, I'll ask around until I do."

He smiled at me, and his attention momentarily shifted to Evaline, who gave him a quick nod. Before I could even react to his quick movements, he got up on his toes and kissed me on my cheek. I caught his blush before he was out of the little makeshift office.

"You two are lovely together. It's good to see Eli around someone that makes him smile. I was starting to wonder if he'd ever find someone to be serious about. At least he never considered Mason as a viable option. That boy needs to grow up quite a bit before he'd be a good romantic interest for anyone," Evaline said as she retook her seat. "Now, why did you want to speak with me this morning?"

I was glad he hadn't ever decided to be with Mason too. That would make things far more complicated than they needed to be. I didn't need to know about the other people that Eli had been with. If I never met them for the rest of my life, I would be perfectly fine with that.

"I'm sure you know how important this place is to Eli. Working with the horses and helping them means the world to him," I began.

She smiled as if she'd known that for years. "Did he ever tell you how we met?"

"He said that he was lost before you found him, but I didn't press him for more than that. I've found that he isn't very forthcoming about his past when he's pushed for information."

Evaline sighed. "He is a stubborn little boy. So, all right, I will tell you his sordid tale. And if he decides to throw a fit, then I'll send him off to do extra barn chores, because I believe in honesty and people being open with each other, especially as they begin to grow a life together as you two seem to be doing. When he was seventeen, he'd already graduated from high school, though only just barely. But finding a place to live and a job were proving to be difficult for him. I found him walking along the road on my way home from the grocery store. He might have been homeless, or he might have been sleeping on someone's couch. I didn't ask. But I needed help, and he promised to do whatever I wanted done. He slept on the couch for a few weeks, and then as we got to know each other, I gave him a room in my house. He worked hard, and he never slacked off once. Do you understand what I'm saying?"

I wasn't sure at all what she was getting at actually. "No, but I am glad to know more about him, as sad as his story is."

But Evaline just shook her head at me as if I was missing the point entirely. "He's not a sad case at all. He's a survivor. He's tough, and he throws himself into what he cares about. He needed a place to belong, and he made this rescue that place for himself. He will always need this rescue. I'm sure of it. So if you're thinking of taking him away from here, I will fight you on that. You may be much younger than me, but I love that boy, and I want what's best for him."

Ah. So that's what she was getting at. I was glad we were on the same page then with our ideas where Eli's future was concerned. Now, if we were matched up as far as what I wanted to talk to her about for the rest of the meeting, I thought this time with her could be considered a great success.

"I have no interest in doing anything of the sort to him actually. I know how devastating losing Green Acres would be for him. That's what I wanted to talk to you about. Green Acres means so much to him that I'd like to try to find a way to support your efforts so that he always has this place. He's told me that once you retire, you've talked about him taking over for you, and I think he would love to do that, once the time comes. I'm here this morning to find out how I can help you. I'll make a donation, which I know will help things temporarily, but there must be more that I can do to help."

She stared at me, then smiled as she reached across the desk and took my hands in hers. "You are a good man with a very good heart. I knew I liked you from the first time we spoke on the phone. Well, tell me, what can you do?"

That was the problem. I didn't have much relevant experience when it came to horses or animal rescues at all. I might have had years of education and decades of experience behind me, but I didn't see how any of it would actually amount to much in her eyes.

"I have a master's degree in business administration from Yale, and many references...."

"Have you ever worked with a nonprofit before?" she asked me.

"Only yours."

"Could you learn the taxes and send out letters requesting grants? I do those tasks right now, and as much as I adore Eli, I think he could use some help with them. I'm not saying he's stupid by any means, but he lacks business sense and sometimes becomes overwhelmed when I put too many papers in front of him."

That was good information to have. I would be doing the taxes, then, assuming we ever filed jointly. Which would mean that we would be married. That was a new and frightening thought, but not as much as I expected it to be. I would spend more time thinking about that later, when we'd been living together for a lot longer than we were now.

"I could learn those tasks," I told her.

"That would be wonderful. Do you think that six months would be an appropriate time frame?"

She'd lost me again. "Six months to learn them? Or what are you hinting at?"

"If you're comfortable with requesting grants and going through a nonprofit's taxes in six months, which would put us at when we need to send our taxes out, then I'll step down. That will give Eli months to get used to being in control more. I hate that Thrall had to die for me to realize that I'm ready to take a few more days off a month. I won't ever entirely step back, but I believe Eli is strong enough to handle this place on his own. And, let's face it, I won't be here forever. It took Thrall's passing for me to realize that I need to start handing over the reins of this place to Eli so that this rescue can continue on after I'm gone."

I loved her idea, and I was sure that when Eli heard it, he would think it was just as wonderful. He would get to run the rescue, and I would be helping him do it while I handled paperwork, which I was good at.

"When would you like me to begin?"

"I'm surprised you're willing to take a job without pay, given your experience. Is it just to be near Eli more often?"

That might have been part of it. And I did want him to be happy and the rescue to succeed so that he'd always have a place here. But money wasn't a factor for me in that equation.

"I do not need to be paid anything for my work at this point in my life if it is something I care about. And Eli is someone I care deeply about, and he loves this rescue very much. That is enough reason for me to want to help you in whatever way I can. I came here hoping that I could find something to do that would allow me to facilitate a change in my life, and I believe you've given me that opportunity."

"Are you able to come back next week so that I can show you the process of asking for grants and trying to get local companies to donate to us or sponsor one of the horses or a new building project?"

She looked so hopeful, as if I was doing something great for her. But really I was the one who was excited to begin. "Yes, that will be fine." I hadn't been this excited to go to work for anyone in years.

We shook hands, and I rose from my seat. "Thank you for your time, and the opportunity to help your rescue. I'll go find Eli and say goodbye to him, and then I'll be on my way."

"Take care of yourself, Grayson. I am so glad we met. That's fate. Do you believe in that?"

I didn't, but she looked so sure of herself that I didn't want to disappoint her. Still, I had the moral code to know better than to lie to an elderly woman, even if it was to make her happy.

"I actually don't. I'm sorry."

She waved her hand at me. "Don't be sorry. And don't you worry about it either. If fate exists, which I believe it does, then it will still be here for you even if you never believe in it. That's how things like this work."

I was sure it would be. "Have a good rest of your day, Evaline."

"You too, dear. I'll see you next week."

I left the office to go searching for Eli, but it actually didn't take me that long to find him since he was heading straight toward me with Mason fawning over him as they walked together. If I was more of a jealous man, I might have cared that Eli's best friend was hanging on him like he was Eli's biggest fan. As it was, I was far more focused on why Eli was holding his wrist against his chest with his other hand wrapped around it protectively.

"What happened?" I asked him.

He shrugged, and though he might have been trying to downplay things for Mason, as he often did for me when he was hurt, I knew enough to look at his eyes. He could hide a lot, but his eyes gave away all of his secrets, and right then I knew how much pain he was in. He was practically screaming it.

"Eli…."

He shook his head, but not at me. "Mason, really, I'm fine. See? Grayson's here. He'll make sure that I get an ice pack. I'll let Evaline know that I got hurt, and then everything will be okay. Go back to work. You don't have to worry so much."

"You sure?" Mason asked him, hesitating.

Eli nodded. "Yeah. Totally sure. I'll see you tomorrow."

"Okay." Mason briefly touched his shoulder, and then Eli and I were alone at the edges of the property.

"I'm taking you to the hospital. There's one not too far from here." I expected some kind of an argument, because I knew how stubborn he could be. But all I got from him was a resigned sigh, and that in itself told me everything I needed to know. He'd gotten hurt, and it was serious enough that he wanted to get it checked out.

"Fine. But I need to tell Evaline what happened first and I don't have health insurance, so we're going to go to a clinic instead of the hospital. No way in hell can I afford an emergency room visit."

I began to argue with him and also tell him that I would be paying for it so I wanted him to have the best care possible, when he walked away from me and headed into the office where Evaline still was. I followed after him and made sure he sat down on the couch. He was too pale to be standing right then.

Eli turned to Evaline. She looked so worried about him, and I understood that intensely as I ran my hand down his back. I knew he was there, and that the injury was likely minor since he was still walking around and coherent, but I needed that physical connection to him right then just to know that he was okay and close to me. It was as if I couldn't stand to have any distance between us. Even an inch was too much space.

"One of the horse's leads got wrapped around my wrist when they reared. I'm sorry that I was careless. It won't happen again. But it hurts enough that I'd like to go get it checked out. Is that okay?"

Evaline pursed her lips at him. "Is that *okay*? Eli! You should already be heading toward a doctor. Go! Next time, text me. Or call me. Or have Mason come tell me that you needed to go. Don't waste time explaining to me that you got hurt when you could be getting patched up. Shoo!"

I wanted to smile at her tone, and I might have if I hadn't been so worried about Eli and she hadn't been so irate. I got him to his feet, and we headed to my car. That he couldn't buckle himself in was a surprise. That he gasped when the seat belt settled across his chest, and his wrist, which he still hadn't moved, bothered me.

"Now that we're alone, tell me how serious it is." I knew where an urgent care clinic wasn't too far from the rescue. I'd passed it on the way coming down, and I headed there now.

"Probably broken. Shit." He was annoyed, but at himself or the horse or the situation as a whole, I wasn't entirely sure.

"How bad is your pain right now?"

He closed his eyes and leaned back against the seat. "Somewhere between cry like a baby and curse like a sailor. Not the worst I've ever been in, but I forgot how much it hurts for these little bones to get messed up. I'd rather get a fractured rib any day, though some people say that hurts more. I find that only really hurts when I breathe too deeply. Or try to laugh. This just hurts all the time." He shook his head, but he kept his eyes closed. "Tell me about your meeting with Evaline. It'll help distract me. What did she want?"

"It's what I wanted actually. I'm going to be doing some work for the rescue."

This time he did open his eyes to look at me as I was pulling into the urgent clinic's parking lot. "I thought there wasn't room in the budget to hire someone, and you've got to be making a lot more than me. I only make fifteen thousand a year. Enough to live on but certainly not enough for you."

I chuckled, and minutes later we were walking into the clinic. He signed in while I spoke to him. "I'm doing the work on a volunteer basis, and you don't need to worry about me and money."

"Could you buy me a pony?" he asked jokingly as we went to sit down in one of the uncomfortable-looking chairs. I rested my arm around his shoulders.

"If you wanted one, I could easily afford to get you a horse." They couldn't be that expensive to care for.

"Right now I'd take a unicorn who could make me less likely to get hurt all the time. I love working at the rescue, but seriously, this getting hurt all the time bit sucks ass."

I chuckled and rubbed his shoulder. He leaned into me, and then I caught him flipping off someone across the room. I hadn't even noticed anyone else in the waiting room with us, but now that he'd pointed out the angry-looking man, who was likely the same age as me, I couldn't help glaring at him. I even turned my head to kiss Eli's hair, for good measure.

"Think he's more pissed off that you're black or we're different ages or we're gay?" Eli asked me.

It could have been all of those actually. I didn't really care. "Maybe he doesn't like people who drive cars. Maybe he's only into trucks."

"And women with breast implants the size of their heads who wear cutoff jeans and cowboy boots," Eli said with a snicker.

The guy had lost interest in us, instead choosing to stare at a TV, so Eli stopped as well. He relaxed against me, and I stroked my hand over his neck and shoulder. "Can I get you anything?"

"A new wrist. Mine is useless."

I smiled and was glad that he still had his sense of humor, even when he was hurting. "I'm serious, Eli. Do you want some water?"

He shook his head. "I'm okay. Thanks. Wish you didn't have to see me so beat up and broken all the time. Seems like I'm always in too much pain lately to really have much fun with."

I kissed the top of his head again. "While I'd love for you to get hurt less, having sex with you isn't the reason I want that. I care about you. I love you. And I worry about you."

He was suddenly tense under my arm. "I'm not quitting the rescue. Straight up, you need to know that right now. Even if a horse kills me someday, I need to be there."

"Shh. Relax. I know that. You've said it. I'd never ask you to give up something you love so much just because of my peace of mind. I have no intention of controlling you or telling you what to do in any way. I'm allowed to worry about you, though, and wish that you were safer, but I know why you do what you do, and being around horses can be dangerous. It likely always will be. You're not working with perfectly trained animals here. I fully understand that. I respect you for what you do, and I wouldn't want you to change that or any part of yourself. Not for the world."

He went silent until a nurse came and got him. I hesitated in the chair, not sure if he'd want me there with him when he went back to see a doctor. But Eli frowned down at me as if he couldn't understand why I was still sitting down.

"Aren't you coming with me? They might poke me with a needle or something. I may need a hand to hold." He smiled at me, and I followed him back, with my hand at the base of his spine.

He was shown to a chair that leaned back, and he got as comfortable as he could as the paper sheet crinkled under him. "I don't like clinics or hospitals," he confided once the nurse had left us alone.

"I don't either. But this is for the best. We want to make sure your wrist isn't too badly damaged."

I moved back as a doctor came in to talk to Eli. An exam, a few X-rays, and a cast for his broken wrist later and we were ready to go. I was glad to be out of there and heading home by the time it was over. And Eli had been so out of it from the pain that he hadn't tried to argue with me, much, when I pulled out a card to pay for his visit.

"You shouldn't have."

"I know."

He looked over at me in the car as I started driving us up to Thornwood. "I could have. I should have."

"No. I like taking care of you. But, if it makes you feel any better, the next time that you break your wrist, I'll let you pay for your own clinic visit."

He grinned. "Deal. What time do you have to leave for the airport?"

I'd actually forgotten all about my client for the next few days. I'd send them an email explaining the situation, or as much of my private life as I was willing to share with a complete stranger. If they didn't like it, then they could hire someone else to restructure their employees. Eli might have been fine. The doctor said that he only needed to take a day off to rest at home but that he wouldn't be riding or working with the horses as long as he had a cast on. I could have gone to work, but I didn't want to leave him when he was hurt.

"I'm not leaving right now."

"I'm sorry. You don't have to stay. I know how important your job is to you. If you're staying just for me, then don't worry about it. I mean, I can handle using one hand for a while, and you were only going to be gone a few days. I can stay with Evaline if you're worried about my driving. I don't want to keep you from doing something just because I'm hurt."

"I'm staying because I want to be around to take care of you, should you need any help. And this job doesn't really need to happen right now. None of them do. Evaline gave me six months to learn what she wants me to so that I can take over the grant writing and the taxes for the rescue. After that time, if I like what I'm doing at the rescue, I intend to stop doing my job entirely. I'm tired of the travel, the people, and, as we've grown closer together, I've realized I don't really like being away from you for days or weeks on end all that much."

Eli grinned at me and blew me a kiss. "Awesome." I fully agreed with his assessment.

I parked us in front of the diner before we went back to my house. Which, admittedly, I was starting to think of being more of our house. He had his bedroom, I had mine, and it was too soon to say out loud to him that it was our house, but that's how I was starting to feel about it. The house had certainly never felt like my house until he started living in it. And I wanted to tell him that, but I was also afraid of scaring him away. I needed to be patient with him and not rush into things where he was concerned. How he'd reacted when I hadn't even said that I loved him yet, but he'd apparently picked up on it, was enough of a clue for me.

"What are we doing here?" Eli asked me.

"I'm starving. Are you hungry at all?" Maybe he was in too much pain to eat.

"I'm in serious need of a milkshake."

That sounded like a good plan to me.

We shared a platter of chicken fingers with french fries and honey mustard sauce, but we ended up each getting our own milkshakes. I hadn't had a milkshake in at least fifteen years, and watching him indulge in his made me want to get my own. I was glad that I did.

There was a cop watching us from a few tables over. I knew his name started with a *T* from the few times I'd seen him around town and heard people talking to him, but more than that I couldn't remember. Why he was staring at us so intently, though, I couldn't imagine. Thornwood was definitely small enough to have some resident homophobic assholes, but I'd hoped they weren't on the police force in the event that I ever needed to call for help.

"Whatcha looking at?" Eli asked me as he munched on his lunch.

I tilted my head in the cop's direction. "There's an officer watching us. I find his attention odd considering that we haven't done anything to warrant such blatant staring."

Eli turned to look at him too, but he wasn't subtle about it. "What's up, Trent?" he called over to him, which made the officer, who I supposed was named Trent, turn away from us and laugh at something the other cops were saying. "He can be a dick, but he's generally harmless."

"How do you know him?" I hadn't thought Eli knew anyone in Thornwood but myself.

Eli chewed on a chicken tender and looked out of the window. "He's…." He turned his attention back to me. "Are you jealous at all? Of people I've been with?"

I frowned. I hadn't ever anticipated knowing any of the people he'd shared a bed with. I wasn't sure how I'd take that. "I don't believe so, but that doesn't extend to you flirting with someone in front of me."

He grinned. "Wouldn't think of it. But Trent's the first guy I met on the app. He was my first everything." He went back to eating. "It's really not that big of a deal," he said between bites of food, which he brought awkwardly to his mouth with his left hand since his right, his dominant one, was in a cast and currently lying in his lap.

"Are you still friends with him?"

For some reason that made Eli laugh. "Not at all. His husband's nice, but Trent's okay. I mean, I won't try to send a bunch of angry squirrels after him or anything like that, but he's not someone I would want over for grilling nights on the weekends. If you were into grilling."

The person who had Eli's virginity? I didn't really want him in my house. I didn't mind that he existed, but I would have been fine never knowing that Trent was his name or that he lived in the same tiny town that I now did.

"Was he good to you?"

Eli cocked his head at me. "He wasn't a jackass, but he wasn't like you are."

I was too interested in what he had to say to eat any more. Eli, on the other hand, didn't seem to have that problem as he ate ravenously. "And how am I?"

"You give a damn. You care. You always let me come first. Sometimes you don't even ask for anything either. It's nice."

That should have been his standard, not his exception, though I did feel good knowing he considered me to be one of his best sexual partners. If not his best. I could be vain and prideful at times, and knowing that someone as kind and attractive as Eli thought I had merits in bed brought out those qualities. I wasn't ashamed to admit that cither.

"You are an easy person to be with," I told him quietly. The fact of the matter was that Eli was my best lover as well. And I'd had a fair number of them.

He snickered. "Did you just say that I was easy?"

I tried to backtrack, but he laughed, and then so did I because I realized he was joking.

After lunch we walked over to the grocery store to get a few essentials, and somehow that landed us in the ice cream aisle as Eli crouched in front of the various flavors of chocolate to make his selection. He glanced up at me with his injured arm dangling between his thighs. "What do you like?"

I wasn't much for ice cream, with the exception of the milkshake I'd just devoured, so I gave him a shrug. "Pick whatever you like. Then we'll go find some actual food."

He settled on a low-quality chocolate chip. I frowned and wondered if he'd be upset if I said anything, but I did want him to know that he could enjoy the more expensive varieties if he wanted to. Groceries were never his responsibility to pay for, even before we'd started dating and he was simply my roommate.

"Do you like that kind?"

"I don't know. I've never tried it before. Do you think it looks awful?" He hesitated instead of simply putting it in the cart as he waited for my answer.

"I don't think it does, but would you rather get the more expensive brand?"

He looked from the ice cream in his hand to the ones still in the case and went back over to them. "You don't mind?" he asked me.

"Not at all. Pick the one that you want most, not which one costs the least."

He gave me a shy, barely there kind of smile before switching out the ice cream he'd picked out for one that cost double but said that it was made with real cream. After that I was able to steer us toward some actual food, where I picked out a spinach soufflé, along with some pierogis.

Eli took them out of the cart to look at them as I chose a few raviolis for us as well. "What are these?" he asked me.

"Pockets of dough with potatoes and cheese in them. Like a ravioli, but not. Sometimes it seems as if every culture has their own version of a pocket of dough with something inside of them. Wontons, raviolis, empanadas, pierogis, samosas, egg rolls...." I turned around to find him still looking at the bag doubtfully. "We'll deep-fry them. You'll like them that way."

That got him to smile, and soon the pierogis were in the shopping cart, and we were headed down the aisle to get some more frozen food. When he stopped in front of the pizza, I wasn't surprised. I wasn't exactly thrilled either. I didn't dislike pizza necessarily, but it wasn't something I was going to seek out.

"What do you like?" he asked me.

"Whatever you want."

He chose a pizza with everything on it, this time one of good quality. I was not looking forward to it, but I knew I'd eat it. He was willing to try pierogis. I could stomach pizza with a dozen different toppings on it with all of those flavors clashing together in my mouth.

My face must have given something away, because as he put the pizza into the cart, he said, "We'll deep-fry it. You'll like it more like that." He winked, and I laughed.

We got milk and orange juice next, and he made a detour after that toward the condom aisle, where he rubbed his hand over his stomach. I wondered if this was a new nervous gesture for him or if he was having trouble deciding.

"Are we running low already?" I asked him.

He shrugged and glanced up at me. "I'm not sure. I didn't check before we left this morning to get to the sanctuary, but I figure since we're here, we might as well get some."

Eli had a point, but there was something I'd been wanting to talk to him about as well. "Are you clean?" I asked him as I ran my fingers lightly down his spine. He nodded instantly and moved closer to the display to start reading a few of the many boxes. I went with him, eager as I was to touch him. "I am too. So why are we still using them?"

"Get proof, and we won't. I'll go get tested as well. We can make a date of it."

He was serious, but I still felt a bit hurt that he wouldn't just take my word for it. "You don't trust me enough to just assume I'm telling you the truth?"

There was no hesitation as he shook his head. He wouldn't apologize for it either, I was sure. And I loved him a little more for that.

"It's my body and my health. I care about you, and I trust you in some ways. But I still want proof before I have unprotected sex with you."

I cupped his chin between my fingers and tilted his head so I could kiss him. "Good answer."

He smirked at me as he pulled back. "I thought you were going to be mad at me for not instantly agreeing to get rid of the condoms and saying it's all fine and everything's okay."

"You want to take care of yourself. I'm not mad about that. I love how smart you are and how you make your own decisions without worrying about what I think. Sometimes, like the food, you'll go with my suggestion, but that's not your normal course of action. I like that about you."

He blushed, and I kissed him again. He grabbed a plain pack of condoms, and we were done shopping after that.

We went home, put the groceries away, and curled up on the couch together. But he seemed antsy. I thought he might have been in pain from his wrist, but he hardly seemed to be paying attention to it as he laid his arm across his stomach while the rest of him was over my lap.

"What's wrong?" I asked him when it was clear that he wasn't paying attention to the crime drama he'd chosen to watch.

He frowned up at me, and I rubbed his chest. His stomach would have been an easier angle for me to get to, but I didn't want to risk hurting his arm while he had it lying there.

"I think I should give Nigel another chance. But if he's mean to me at all and you don't tell him to take a step back and knock it the hell off, you're sleeping on your own tonight."

I moved my hand to his cheek. He opened his mouth when I brought my thumb over his lips while I thought, but my thoughts were quickly interrupted by the sensation of him sucking gently on my thumb as if he wanted to remind me just how good he was with his mouth if I did screw up when Nigel was here. I didn't need the reminder. I liked every part of him, but mostly his mind and his heart.

"Why would you want to risk subjecting yourself to him again?" I pulled my thumb out of his mouth with a little pop so that he could answer me.

He put his good hand over mine on his chest. "He's your best friend. Right? I wouldn't be okay with it if you and Mason didn't get along, so maybe it's important that Nigel and I can be in the same room together. I'm willing to give him another chance, especially now that he can see that I'm not just your live-in fuck toy but that I actually matter to you."

166

His reasons made sense, but I did not like it when he talked about himself like that. "You were never a fuck toy with me. I always wanted to know more about you, and I always wanted to push you to share more of yourself with me, but I was afraid if I pushed you too hard you'd simply walk away from me, and that would be the end of us."

Eli nodded, and I knew my suspicions were right. "I'm not good at letting people into my life. As you've probably already been able to tell." Given how his own mother chose someone else over taking care of her son, I didn't blame him at all for his refusal to get close to most people. "So, you're right, if you had pushed me too hard, I would have stopped talking to you. But that would have been on me, not on you. And it's still scary sometimes how close I've let you get to me already."

"I'm sure it is. And hopefully someday I'll be able to convince you that I don't want to hurt you at all."

He blew me a kiss. "Unless I ask you to, of course."

"Eli…." We'd been having a serious conversation, and he was bringing sex into it. I wasn't pleased by that turn in the conversation.

He rolled off my lap so that he was standing. "I know. I know. Call Nigel or text him or whatever you two do and ask him to come over tonight. We can have those pierogis you promised me I wouldn't hate."

"Are you sure you want to see him so soon?"

Eli went into the kitchen and awkwardly poured himself a glass of milk with one hand. I could have helped, and maybe I should have, but I saw his dark look as soon as I got off the couch, warning me away from doing just that. He was independent. I knew that, and I could respect that about him. But it was also hard not to rush in and take care of him when he was hurt.

"Might as well. Right? He's your best friend. That's not going to stop being the case anytime soon unless he does something to seriously fuck it all up, and that won't be because of me. He might as well start getting used to me being in your life, and I can put up with him being all pompous." He pranced a bit, making fun of Nigel. And I probably shouldn't have laughed at that, but I did. Eli smiled at me, and I took out my phone to make the call.

CHAPTER SEVENTEEN

Eli

NIGEL CAME over at close to seven that night. Grayson had changed into a pair of dark slacks and a pale green button-down shirt. I wasn't sure why he'd made the effort. Weren't friends supposed to be fine with whatever the hell the other person had on at the time? That's what I always thought anyway. But Grayson had actually dressed up for Nigel, and Nigel was wearing a suit. I sipped my shiraz and tried to pay attention to them as they talked about business and money and the new car that Nigel wanted. And I was really glad Grayson wasn't this dull.

"You know, Grayson, these pierogis would be much better if you'd made them in the traditional way in a skillet with some butter and some onions and a good tablespoon of sour cream overtop," Nigel was saying. It was really the only bit of the conversation that had caught my attention at all, and I shifted my gaze to Grayson. I didn't know anything about pierogis, but it made me really happy that he would make them like this just for me, since he knew how much I liked fried food. I decided to say more than two words for the first time since Nigel had come through the front door.

I met Nigel's gaze head-on and smiled at him. "He made them like this for me since it's my first time having them. And plus, if I'd known how they were supposed to be made, I wouldn't have eaten them. I don't like onions."

Grayson rubbed my thigh under the table as he sipped his wine to hide his smile. "Really? I didn't know that. Even if they're fried?"

"Even then. But I don't mind kissing you after you've had some." I caught Nigel rolling his eyes as I leaned over and kissed Grayson on his cheek.

"He's cheeky," Nigel said as if I wasn't sitting two feet away from him.

I cocked my head to the side and decided to play dumb. "Grayson, is he complimenting me on my ass? That's so sweet of him." I reached across the table and touched Nigel's hand. "Thank you. I've worked hard on my best feature."

As I pulled back, Grayson was snorting into his wine. "Behave," he told me, though he was grinning.

He was right. I couldn't very well expect Nigel to be nicer to me if I was willing to be such a jerk to him. But it was hard to hold back when Nigel was sitting there acting all high and mighty with his damn pinky sticking out as he sipped wine that really wasn't that good. I would have preferred to have orange juice than this stuff. But I did have to hand it to Grayson; he was right about the pierogis. I liked deep-fried pockets of cheese and mashed potatoes. I could have used something to dip them in, though.

"Grayson," Nigel began as he recovered from whatever stupor I'd put him in with my words. "Surely you can see how absolutely uncultured he is. The sex probably is fantastic by the looks of him, but how could it ever be anything more than that?"

I looked at Grayson to see if he'd say anything. If he didn't I wouldn't be storming down to Caleb's to spend time with Hawk again, but he would absolutely be sleeping alone and cold in his own bed tonight.

Grayson put down his wine and leaned forward. I sipped from my glass and pretended the taste didn't make me want to hurl. If Grayson stood up for me, I wouldn't really be able to help my grin. But if he didn't, I had no intention of letting Grayson know just how upset he would make me while Nigel was there to witness it. I didn't really like him being there to begin with. I wasn't going to let him see my pain, hurt, and anger too.

"Nigel," he began. "You're my best friend. And Eli is the man I'm in love with. Try harder if you want to remain my friend. It's not asking too much that you refrain from saying rude things either to him or about him whether you're in his presence or not."

I put my wineglass down and smiled over at Grayson.

"How'd I do?" he asked me.

My smile turned into a wide grin. "Just fine. You're getting laid tonight, by the way."

He laughed, and we both turned our attention back to Nigel. I didn't like him in the least, but he was Grayson's best friend, so I wanted him to stay in Grayson's life if only for that reason. And then I could think to myself about how Grayson needed better friends, and Nigel needed to get off his damn high horse and come back to reality with the rest of us lowlife scum.

Nigel took a deep drink of his wine, and I wondered if he had taste buds at all or if nasty-tasting wine had gotten rid of them for him. Considering the wine, not having any taste buds was probably a blessing if that was his thing. If not, my next option was that he was plain crazy, because he really needed to choose a wine that didn't taste disgusting.

"Are you sure about this?" Nigel asked Grayson, again as if I wasn't sitting right there. Was I invisible? Nope. But Nigel was good at making me feel like I suddenly was. "He's so…."

He waved his hand at me, and I waited for him to continue on with whatever bullshit reason he had now of why Grayson shouldn't even want to look at me. Oh, no, looking at me was fine. So was screwing me apparently. But heaven forbid Grayson actually wanted something more to do with me beyond my mouth and ass. I really needed to pull back on my anger before I ended up tossing the rest of my mostly full glass of wine into Nigel's face.

"White." Nigel finally decided on the perfect insult. Probably at least in his mind.

And I just stared at him, as did Grayson, because really? Out of all the insults he could have thrown at me and all the problems he could have found with me, he decided to go with race? I laughed. I couldn't help it.

"Holy shit. You're racist," I said as I got up from the table to go get a second helping of the fried pockets of mashed potato goodness. I sat right back down next to Grayson and decided to screw forks. I'd eat with my fingers. Apparently my manners, my low social class, my age, my lack of money and education— none of it mattered as much as the fact that I was white. And I couldn't help that, so I decided to say fuck it all and act like I wanted to for the rest of the night.

Grayson took a lot longer to recover than I did. "Nigel, thank you for coming over tonight. I'm glad that I got to see how you really are. I'm just surprised I didn't realize before. I'd like you to leave now."

Without a word Nigel tossed down his napkin and stormed out of the house. He even slammed the door behind him like he was somehow insulted that Grayson had chosen me over him, when really it was that Grayson had chosen to be a decent person, instead of a racist asshole, unlike his best friend.

Grayson ran his hands over his face before he turned back to me. I was licking mashed potatoes off my fingertips. "I am so sorry about that. I had no idea, and I feel like an idiot. I should have never let him near you."

"I'm sorry your best friend turned out to be a douchebag. Maybe once you start working at the rescue, you'll meet some other guys who are much nicer. They're all about my age so fair warning on that."

"You wouldn't be jealous if I made friends with some people your age?"

Was I supposed to be? "Um… no? Why would I be?" Then it hit me. "Oh! You think that I'd assume you're cheating! That makes much more sense now. And no, I wouldn't mind. And if you cheated, then you cheated. I'd only be upset that you didn't tell me you weren't happy with whatever dating thing we're doing. I value honesty more than I want to go around stalking you and worrying about who you're with constantly. You deleted the app. That's enough for me. If you wanted to cheat, there are far easier ways to do it than to try to hook up with guys that I work with, where I would definitely find out because everyone there talks like crazy."

He smiled and kissed me softly. Which was nice, and I liked every way that he wanted to kiss me, but I really wanted more than that from him right then.

"Did you get enough to eat?" I asked him as I moved my good hand to his thigh and leaned in closer to him.

"Yes. I think I did."

He was grinning at me now too as if he knew where I was going with this. "And are you all done with the disgusting wine Nigel brought over?"

"I see you didn't like it much either."

I took his hand and brought him up from his chair. He locked the front door, and we left the dishes as they were. We could clean up later. I laced my fingers with his as we went upstairs to his bedroom.

I wanted to be all sexy as I stripped down for him, but trying to undress with one hand was crap. I ended up getting stuck with my T-shirt halfway off my head and my bad arm trapped in it.

"Ow, ow, shit, ow," I grumbled until Grayson, laughing, came over to help me.

"It was a good show up until that point," he said as he helped me get out of the shirt. My pants were much easier to take care of, and then I was just in my boot socks, which really weren't that sexy.

I sat down on the edge of his bed to take them off. "Yeah, yeah. Let's hope that you never break your wrist."

"Since I don't often play with crazy, unpredictable horses I don't think that will be anything that you have to be worried about."

He was naked a few minutes later, and I smiled up at him as he stepped between my thighs and offered himself to me. I'd sucked him plenty of times, but that was before everything else. And this was different. I kissed his stomach and ran my hands down his sides. His short hairs tickled my nose as I brushed my mouth over his dark skin. I loved how dark he was and how beautiful he was, like a deep black horse whose color was so much more interesting up close.

I kissed his base as the tip of his cock slid against my throat, leaving a trail of wetness in its wake. I didn't mind. I actually kind of liked the taste of him.

I stroked him first and smiled as his hands went to my shoulders and the back of my head. That's why I didn't often suck people. Because everyone seemed so interested in trying to choke me with their cocks, like that somehow made them better, cooler, or more powerful, knowing that they could gag someone. I thought that it made them jackasses. But Grayson only ran his fingers through my hair as I slid my hand over his cock. I wanted to have my other hand free to play with his balls, but that wasn't going to happen for a while because of the damn cast.

I licked him from his base to his tip, then continued to gently stroke him while I dipped my head to lap at his balls. His hair there was trimmed short. I'd been with guys who shaved themselves clean, and I'd been with guys who looked like they had no idea that razors even existed. I liked it like this, where I knew Grayson cared about his appearance, but he wasn't obsessive over it. There were plenty of other things for him to be neurotic over besides how hairy his balls were.

He helped me start the condom, since it would have been pretty hard to do without the use of my other hand, and then I slid my mouth carefully over his length. He touched the back of my throat, but since he wasn't holding me down or even guiding me at all, I could pull away instantly. I really hated the condom, though. It was a barrier between us when I didn't want anything there ever again. And it annoyed me to no end that I couldn't feel his thick veins under my tongue as I took him between my lips.

I lay back shortly after that, and he covered me with his body just as we'd done in the woods. I kept my hurt arm above my head so that it would stay out of the way. I was in pain now, and while the clinic had given me pain pills, I hadn't taken any. But I'd get some later. I didn't want to stop now just to go pop some pills and come right back into the moment. That seemed like far too much work, especially when I had Grayson kissing me and sliding against me with his cock. He was teasing me, and I loved it, but I wanted more from him. I brought my thighs up around his hips and felt him reach down to my hole. Maybe he thought he needed to remove my plug for me, since I hadn't before I'd sat on the bed, but when I felt his fingers against my hole, he smiled down at me.

"You're not wearing it," he said.

"Only ever did because it was a way to keep guys from rushing to get their dicks in me before I was ready. I realized that I don't have to do that with you."

He kissed me on my forehead. "You never, ever wore it because you liked how it felt?"

"Not really. I mean, sometimes, when I was riding it felt really good. But most of the time it was there so that I was already stretched, and I made sure that the guys couldn't hurt me. A few of them thought it made me a slut, since I was always ready for sex, but I preferred that to the times I hadn't worn it before realizing that I needed it. Some guys were fine, but some can be serious dicks about wanting sex when they want it and not when I was ready for it. And you know I like some pain, but I draw the line at pushing in before I'm ready to take a cock."

I caught Grayson staring. Then he kissed me long and slow. Lube came next, and I waited as he stretched me. He took minutes making sure I was okay and asking me the whole time that he was doing it if he was hurting me. Sometimes he wasn't even stretching me. Sometimes he'd just run his fingers around my hole and tease me like it was kind of a damn game. I was really starting to miss my plug by the time he stopped teasing me and slid his cock up against my hole.

There was pressure as he pushed into me, but there was no pain to go with it. He'd done a good job of getting me ready. I just wanted him to hurry up now and fuck me. That would be really nice. But Grayson seemed determined to go slow as he slid inside of me like neither one of us was in any kind of a rush. He rained kisses down over my cheeks and chin, and I gasped under him as he pushed inside of me with such glacial speed that I was ready to start begging before he ever got deep in me.

Thankfully he didn't make me wait too much longer before he was all the way in me, and I had my legs clamped around his hips as he started to really work me. I kept having to remind myself not to reach over with my bad hand to touch his shoulder like I normally did. I liked having his muscles move under my fingers. He had wide shoulders. I'd thought he was a linebacker or something at first. He was built like it. And I loved that about him too. He was big and powerful, and when he really started to fuck me, I could always feel that part of him. Sure he dealt with papers all day and sat at a desk when he was at work, but when he wasn't, there was something about him that said that he could have done anything with his life, and he still had so much potential wrapped up in him.

He gasped out my name with each hard stroke into me, and I closed my eyes as I clung to him. His tight hairs tickled my belly and my cock, and I bit down on the inside of my cheek to keep from coming before I was ready. I wanted more time with him. I wanted hours more, just like this, where there was nothing else in my world except for Grayson and his impossibly soft bed underneath me.

"Marry me," he whispered against my neck in between lightly biting me.

I opened my eyes and glared at him. "Excuse me?"

He didn't even falter in his pace as he leaned up on his hands to loom over me. "You heard what I said. Marry me. Please?"

"Fuck no." I laughed at him, which instantly made him frown.

"Why not? We love each other. I love having you here. We're great together."

While all of that was true, he was missing the bigger picture. "You can't just ask someone to marry you when you're balls deep in their ass. That's not how it's done. Ask me again later."

"Would you say yes if I asked you properly, then?"

I grinned and looked away from him as he tried to kiss my mouth but only got my cheek. "Maybe. Depends on how you ask. It can't be anything ridiculous like what you just did."

He laughed, and I gave him my mouth this time. We kept kissing, and then there was less kissing as his speed fell apart

177

and his rhythm went to shit. He was close, and my thoughts were circling around marriage and marriage to Grayson and what was marriage like and did I have any right to be married to someone when I was still trying to figure out what, exactly, love was since it wasn't what I'd always thought it was.

Grayson bit my lower lip, snapping me out of my racing, maddening thoughts. I was back in the moment with him within an instant and coming only minutes after that as he grabbed my cock between us and stroked my orgasm out of me.

As soon as I was done, he pulled out of my ass, tossed the condom aside, and came over my hips and stomach, mixing our come together and making me smile. We always did make such an absolute mess.

He was gasping for air as he lay down next to me on the bed and put his arm across my stomach, right where the bulk of our combined come was.

"I need a shower," I said with a groan. But I definitely was not going to be getting up to go get one anytime soon.

"I'm sorry I asked you," he quietly told me once he'd regained the ability to speak coherently and not just gasp out my name and fuck mixed together as he came.

"Are you regretting wanting to marry me already? Because it's kind of shitty to do take-backs on something like that."

He was quick to shake his head and move closer to my side. I was relieved that he wasn't saying that. Marriage was a terrifying concept for me, but if he had already been ready to call it off, I knew I probably would have cried, and I really didn't cry all that often. I couldn't remember the last time I had. I'd been close today, with the pain, and without sex there to cloud up all my thoughts and make me forget about it, the throbbing in my wrist was back with a vengeance. I needed to take some pills, too, to go with my shower.

"I should not have asked you like that, but I don't regret wanting to spend the rest of my life with you. I love you, but tonight sealed it for me. And don't you dare ask me if it was because of the sex that we just had, because not everything in life is about sex."

He knew me too well, because I was absolutely about to make that joke. "Then was it when Nigel was here and being an asshole?"

Grayson kissed me on my sweaty temple. I was surprised he didn't make a face at the grossness of that. "No, it was actually while we were grocery shopping. You stopped and turned to me and told me we could deep-fry the pizza to make me like it more. You were joking, and I knew I loved you so much right then, and I didn't want to ever stop seeing you smile at me like that."

I swallowed deeply and gave him what I hoped was that same smile, though I really wished someone had gotten a picture of us in that moment because I wanted to practice that smile all the time until it was the only one that I ever gave to him.

"My answer is yes."

CAITLIN RICCI was fortunate growing up to be surrounded by family and teachers who encouraged her love of reading. She has always been a voracious reader and that love of the written word easily morphed into a passion for writing. If she isn't writing, she can usually be found studying as she works toward her counseling degree. She comes from a military family, and the men and women of the armed forces are close to her heart. She also enjoys gardening, hiking, and horseback riding in the Colorado Rockies she calls home with her wonderful fiancé and their two dogs. Her belief that there is no one true path to happily ever after runs deeply through all of her stories.

Website: www.CaitlinRicci.com

One
More
Time

A Thornwood Novel

Caitlin Ricci

A Thornwood Novel

Wanting to start over after breaking off a relationship with his married boss, Caleb Robinson is happy to move from Los Angeles to Thornwood, Colorado. He can barely find the town on a map, which is just the kind of place Caleb needs. He's not looking for a relationship, and Thornwood looks to be the perfect place to get lost in his art. But when Thornwood's local police officer, Trent Williams, knocks on Caleb's front door, both men have an instant attraction to each other, and Caleb's plans for solitude might have to change.

But he soon learns that Trent is a legendary one-night-stand man for a very special reason. His boyfriend has been kept on life support for the past five years after a serious skiing accident. Even though Simon isn't expected to wake up and Trent says he's trying to get past him, he won't entertain anything that comes close to commitment. As compelling as their attraction is, Caleb doesn't want to be just another hook-up, and he won't be the other man. But Trent isn't sure he can risk the pain of losing someone else he cares about, no matter how intense the chemistry between him and Caleb.

www.dreamspinnerpress.com

A Thornwood Novel

About
Last
Night

Caitlin Ricci

A Thornwood Novel

Before jumping into his first semester of college, Thomas Maloney decides to lose his virginity at a party to a stranger he's sure he'll never see again. Only the next day, he's surprised to learn the same one-night stand will be sharing his dorm room. Thomas considers himself lucky, but his new roommate—not so much.

Closeted as they come, football jock Remington "Rem" Daniels is on track for a shot at the pros. Rem tries to play it cool and avoid falling for the confidently gay Thomas, which could hurt his chances. Dealing with their constant need to get in bed together wouldn't be so hard if Rem didn't have a girlfriend and Thomas didn't have a conscience.

When she delivers news that will change Rem's life forever, Thomas knows it's time to move back home to Thornwood, Colorado. But neither the distance nor knowing Rem belongs to someone else helps Thomas get over him. Rem's feelings haven't changed either. When it comes down to love or football, Rem will have to make the hardest choice of his life and hope Thomas will still be waiting for him when he does.

www.dreamspinnerpress.com

KARA NASH & CAITLIN RICCI

DARE
TO RISK

DARE: BOOK ONE

Dare: Book One

For successful businessman Bran Wilson, selling the large Montana dairy farm that has been in his family for generations is an easy decision. He hates the farm, the land, even the cows, and wants nothing to do with any of it. But there's a glitch in his plan: a stubborn cowboy from New Zealand who is as sexy as he is aggravating.

Kaden Barker loves the Wilson farm, and respected Bran's grandfather up until the day he died. With his two best friends, he's taken over working the farm and caring for the cows, and he'd happily spend the rest of his days doing it.

When Bran charges into his life, telling him he's selling the farm and there's nothing Kaden, or his friends, can do about it, the animosity between them is instant. But so is the attraction, and only one extreme can win out.

www.dreamspinnerpress.com

reckless

caitlin ricci

When his best friend, Lee, offered him his sub as part of a bet, Colton Prier never expected more than a clean condo from the boy. But Tate Nicholson is well-trained, eager , and he likes rope play as much as Colton enjoys tying him up. It should have ended after one night, but they begin meeting in secret, and Colton can't stop thinking about Tate. It's a betrayal of his friendship with Lee to fall in love with Tate, but Colton can't help wanting the sub for himself.

He's not alone in his feelings, either. Tate thought he was happy with Lee. Not completely fulfilled, but happy enough. But as he spends more time with Colton, he realizes Lee isn't capable of giving him what he wants anyway. Lee demands his full submission, but Tate doesn't want to be a lifestyle sub. Colton expects his obedience at times but gives him his freedom more often than not, which is more in line with what Tate wants.

When Tate really needs his Dom and Lee isn't around to help him, he reaches the tipping point and needs to choose who he wants to give his submission to, and to accept the consequences of his choice when he does.

www.dreamspinnerpress.com

CAITLIN RICCI

TO THE
HIGHEST
BIDDER

A Planet Called Wish: Book One

The Intergalactic Star Pilot Academy has accepted Thierry Leroux into the elite class of sky year 2231. But the academy comes with a hefty price tag, and there's no way he, a poor Sythe orphan, has the credits the academy requires. Thierry's brother, Corbin, a high-class companion, suggests Thierry sell his virginity for the cost of tuition. It seems like a ridiculous idea, but it may be Thierry's only shot, so Thierry asks Corbin to arrange a meeting on the pleasure planet of Wish.

On Wish, Thierry meets Corbin's boss, Monroe, and they agree to auction off Thierry's virginity. Thierry is grateful to the masked buyer he knows only as "Dragonfly," and Dragonfly is gentle, making Thierry's first time a good memory. When Dragonfly requests to see him again, and pay for the pleasure, Thierry returns to Wish. But in this game, falling in love is dangerous for the heart, and Thierry might not like the man behind the mask.

www.dreamspinnerpress.com

www.ingramcontent.com/pod-product-compliance
Lightning Source LLC
Chambersburg PA
CBHW060102260626
47160CB00005B/1761